HER COWBOY BILLIONAIRE BODYGUARD

CHRISTMAS IN CORAL CANYON, A WHITTAKER BROTHERS NOVEL, BOOK 4

LIZ ISAACSON

ISBN-13: 978-1729276143

ONE

BEAU WHITTAKER RESISTED the urge to reach up and brush the tiny hairs from the back of his neck. Celia always swatted his hand away when he did, and she'd clean him up anyway. But they sure did itch.

He supposed he should be used to all the itching when it came to hair, as he'd grown a full beard over the course of the last ten months, and he only let Celia shave the back and sides of his head to maintain some sort of respect when he went down the canyon to church. Or maybe he did it for his mother, so she wouldn't reprimand him for letting himself totally turn into a recluse. Or had she said hermit?

It didn't matter. Beau was tired of defending himself. With Andrew out of the lodge now, and living with his new wife in town, someone needed to live at Whiskey Mountain Lodge and take care of the horses. So what if Beau had let his hair grow out in the process? Didn't mean he'd cut himself off from society.

Even if he had.

Celia hummed as she kept the clippers running along his scalp. Across the counter, a pot of soup bubbled, giving off the scent of chicken broth and cooked carrots and freshly made pasta. The only thing that could cover the mouth-watering smell of Celia's town-famous chicken noodle soup was the bread she served with it.

The bowl holding the proofing dough sat beside the stove, and Beau couldn't wait until his haircut was finished. Then he could get these itchy hairs off his neck, and Celia would start kneading and forming rolls. Once he showered and slicked some gel through his hair, the scent of freshly baked bread would fill this kitchen.

And then, only a bit after that, L. Rhett would arrive. Beau's muscles bunched at the thought. He knew whoever had been emailing him these past few weeks had been using a pseudonym, as well as a brand new email account. He wasn't even sure if he was meeting a man or a woman, which was why he'd asked his oldest brother, Graham, to come to the lodge a few minutes before this Rhett person was set to arrive.

Beau hoped the case would be worthwhile, as he hadn't done much but grow hair and ride horses for a few months now. At the same time, those two things had been exactly what he'd needed in his life, to soothe his ego and to calm his ragged soul. Somehow, sitting in church every week hadn't done that, as there were so many female eyes watching him. Filled with sympathy at what had happened with his last case —and the woman at the center of it he'd let into his heart.

He exhaled, wishing he could find all the pieces of his

most vital organ, and held completely still while Celia finished his haircut.

"There you go," she finally said, whipping the brush across his neck and ears. She unpinned the drape from around his neck, and he stood to face her.

"Thank you, Celia."

"Do you want to eat now or after you shower?"

"After." He clenched his fist so he wouldn't reach up to touch his neck. "And Graham's coming over."

"Don't I know it? He's texted me five times about sending soup home for his family." Celia gave a light laugh and shook her head. "It's a miracle they all haven't starved."

Beau chuckled too and headed down the hall and into the master bedroom. Every one of his brothers had lived in this room at some point over the last few years, but Beau had added the most to the room.

He'd put up pictures of their family, asked Annie to get him some real paintings of the area from local artists, and in the middle of it all, he'd placed a picture of his mom and dad on the day they got married.

He glanced at the photograph now, a twinge of missing racing through him at the familiar face he found on his dad. It was the same one he saw every time he looked into a mirror. Well, before the beard, at least.

Beau paused to look at his mother. Only eighteen when she married his dad, Beau's mother was the strongest person he knew. She'd raised four boys almost alone as her husband built the largest energy company in Wyoming and ran it for fourteen hours a day, seven days a week.

He was the only brother who'd never left Coral Canyon,

except for a few years to finish law school, and he was the only one who was here the day his dad died.

He ran his fingers along the top of the metal picture frame and sighed, wondering if this meeting was a good idea or not. Beau thought himself a good judge of character, even when the only communication he'd had was through email. And whoever had been conversing with him was in a desperate state.

"Desperate people do desperate things," he muttered to himself as he went to shower. When he returned to the kitchen, complete with his cowboy hat and boots, Graham sat at the counter along with a bowl of soup and three buttered rolls.

"You're early," Beau said, settling onto a barstool beside his brother.

"Mm," Graham said, his mouth full of food and rendering him unable to talk.

But when Celia put a steaming bowl of soup and a plate of rolls in front of Beau, he decided talking was quite over-rated too. Especially when there was eating to be done.

Graham finished before him, and asked, "So who's coming over?"

Beau kept chewing as he tried to figure out how to answer his brother. After swallowing, he said, "Hopefully a new client."

"And you need me here for that?"

"She's obviously not telling me who she really is."

"Then how do you know it's a woman?" The wind rattled the windows behind them in the dining room.

"I don't. I just have a feeling," Beau said. "She wouldn't

show me her case, but insisted that we meet to go over things." He glanced at the blue numbers on the microwave. "She should be here soon."

Graham shook his head and reached for his fourth roll. "If you think it's a woman, what am I doing here?"

"Getting dinner for your family." Beau elbowed him slightly and dunked a piece of his bread in his soup. "And taking Daisy for a couple of days, remember?"

"Oh, right." He glanced around for Beau's Rottweiler. She perked up from her dog bed in the corner of the kitchen. "I guess Bailey needs to draw her for art." He sounded less than thrilled to have a second dog, even for a few days. "I'm not sure why Bear isn't good enough."

"Too old," Beau joked. "How are Laney and the kids?"

"Just fine," Graham said. Beau saw them all the time anyway, especially now that he lived out at the lodge.

Jealousy touched Beau for just a moment. There, then gone. He wanted a house full of kids, like the one he'd grown up in. His mother kept telling him he had plenty of time, but he was almost twice her age when she'd gotten married, and he couldn't even entice a scared woman to stay in town and give their relationship a chance.

Oh, no. Deirdre had chosen her old life down in Colorado over Beau.

His chest pinched and he took an enormous bite of his roll, hoping to quell it. He finished eating, and he and Graham put their dishes in the dishwasher. He'd just stepped into the living room and switched on the fireplace when knocking sounded on the front door.

Graham, who'd just sank into the couch, stood again and met Beau's eyes. "I guess that's her."

Beau ran his hands over his beard and straightened his shoulders. He'd met hundreds of clients over the years, but for some reason this one felt different. He didn't get a lot of anonymity in Coral Canyon, as everyone knew everyone else's business. But this person wasn't from Coral Canyon, he knew that much.

After all, Graham was a tech genius, and he'd tracked the email address to an IP server out of Jackson Hole. Only an hour away, Jackson was at least four times as big as Coral Canyon, with plenty of tourists to gossip about.

He strode over to the door and opened it, Graham right beside him. Together, they stood shoulder to shoulder, filling the doorway and creating a very physical barrier to whoever stood on the stoop.

Sure enough, a woman stood there, haloed in the porch light.

Beau stared as he drank in her long, almost white hair, slight frame, and fair features. She sucked in a breath, her blue eyes turning cold at the same time she deftly reached into her purse and pulled out a canister. She expertly positioned her finger on the top and said, "Who are you?"

Beau couldn't speak, and he wasn't even sure why. His muscles had cinched at the sight of the pepper spray, but really it was this woman's beauty that had rendered him mute and still.

"You rang our doorbell," Graham said easily, leaning his shoulder into the doorframe on his side. Beau still couldn't so much as move, or even blink.

"Which one of you is Beau Whittaker?"

Graham hooked his thumb at Beau. "That'd be him."

Beau lifted his arm, but he didn't have any conscious thought about it. Why couldn't he get his voice to work? He'd never been tongue-tied in all of his thirty-four years, but this woman had stolen his very words from him.

The woman glanced over her shoulder and apparently decided that nothing was going to jump out and attack her, as her finger slipped off the nozzle of the canister.

Graham elbowed Beau in the ribs, which made him go, "Oof," and curl into himself protectively. He glared at his brother, and Graham lifted his eyebrows and chin-nodded toward the beautiful woman still standing on their doorstep.

Beau's face heated, and he managed to take a step backward. "I'm Beau Whittaker," he said, extending his hand for the woman to shake. His skin tingled in anticipation of touching her, and he promptly commanded himself to calm down. "You must be L. Rhett?"

Her eyes flew to his, and he realized in that moment that she'd forgotten the fake name she'd used in her correspondence with him.

Didn't matter. Beau would be getting this woman's real name and phone number, and his prayers that he'd get this new case shifted to an entirely different level, for an entirely different reason.

TWO

LILY EVERETT HAD TAKEN her finger off the nozzle of her pepper spray, but she hadn't committed to putting it fully away. Unsure as to why, she reached out with her other hand and shook Beau's.

He was a big bear of a man, just like his email had said. If bears wore big, black cowboy hats, that was. Which he did, and he looked pretty amazing doing it.

Problem was, the other man standing next to him also wore a cowboy hat and stood easily as wide, equally as bear-like. She pumped Beau's hand a couple of times, glad her father had taught her how to give a proper handshake before flying across the ocean to the Middle East, where he conducted business with his oil company.

"This is my brother, Graham," Beau said. "He just came up for a quick bite to eat." Beau turned to Graham. "I'm sure Celia has your food ready to take down to your family."

Lily didn't miss the hidden message beneath Beau's

words, and she released his hand and looked at his brother simultaneously.

"Nice to meet you," Graham said as if he hadn't gotten the hint that Beau wanted him to leave. "And you are...?"

Both brothers stood there, watching her, but Lily really didn't want to give her name. *They've already stared you down,* she thought, and they hadn't exclaimed or sucked in their breath as they recognized her. Nothing.

"Lily Everett," she finally said, shifting her feet back as if expecting to be hit with their realizations.

"Well, c'mon in," Beau said, stepping back. "We're not going to talk on the porch."

Lily had no sooner stepped into the huge lodge before a woman appeared in the doorway. "I'm headed out, boys. Graham, your food is on the counter." Her eyes landed on Lily, and she smiled for two moments before recognition lit her eyes. "Oh, hello. Sorry, I didn't see you there."

Lily's heart thumped in her chest, sounding like a bass drum in her ears, while she waited for the woman to exclaim over who she was, and which song was her favorite. Then the questions came—*how do you come up with the lyrics for the songs? Are your sisters as beautiful as you? Who taught you to play the piano?*

But the woman just smiled and said, "I'm Celia, but I'm also leaving," as she slipped past the two brothers and past Lily before pulling the front door closed behind her.

"You can put that pepper spray away," Beau said. "I'm not going to bite, and my brother is leaving."

"Oh, right." Graham sprang toward the doorway Celia had come through, leaving Lily alone with Beau. She'd met thousands of people in her life, and she couldn't sense a single ounce of danger surrounding him. So he was a great big *teddy* bear of a man, and Lily couldn't help the way her heart started thumping again.

This time, it wasn't over fear of being discovered for who she was. It was because he stirred something in her that had been dormant for many years. Something Lily had never expected to be so much as disturbed again.

And it's not now, she told herself. *Don't be ridiculous.* She needed Beau's help to get Kent off her back once and for all. She was not interested in the man for much more than his legal skills—and he was the best in the surrounding five states, if her research was correct.

"Would you like to sit?" He chose a chair near the fireplace, which flickered with false flames.

She perched on the edge of the couch across from him, a large, square coffee table between them. Slipping the pepper spray back into her purse, she crossed her legs and peered at Beau. "Thank you for meeting with me."

"Oh, the only things keepin' me busy around here are a few horses." He smiled at her, a warm, made-of-honey smile that helped her relax another notch. He looked like the type of man who could break a horse in a single afternoon.

He startled just a bit, a little flinch, and cleared his throat. "Did you bring your case files?" Beau glanced to her purse, which certainly wasn't large enough for the files he needed. All at once, Lily remembered why she was there and it wasn't to meet a man or get a date.

It was to get her dirty, no-good, cheating ex-husband out of her life for good.

"I just wanted to meet," she said, finding her voice. "If I decide to hire you, then you'll have full access to my files."

"All right," he said easily as if he had conversations like this every evening. Maybe he did, but Lily certainly didn't, and though this was probably one of the most expensive couches she'd ever sat on, she shifted and couldn't find a comfortable spot.

Clearly this Beau Whittaker had some money of his own. The thought actually appealed to Lily quite a lot, as she'd had her fair share of "suitors" who were only interested in her to get closer to her bank account.

Like Kent.

"So what do you need to know, Miss Lily?" Beau relaxed further into his chair, almost like he was fixing to take a nap. With the way the house smelled like warm bread and chicken broth, Lily could see why.

"I'm wondering if you can tell me a little bit about your-self," she said, putting a wall between her and everything else. She'd perfected such things over the years, as she needed to appear to love her fans but also keep them at arm's distance. She had to seem like she adored being on stage even when her heart was broken, or she had a terrible head cold, or she hadn't slept in days.

Oh, yes, Lily Everett could perform and pretend better than almost anyone. And she could ignore these twittering feelings in her stomach and focus on the real reason she'd come all the way to Coral Canyon and then up another canyon to meet this man. This lawyer. And weren't all lawyers sharks? Kent certainly had been.

"Let's see," Beau said. "I'm the youngest of four brothers.

Graham, he's the oldest." His voice settled into an easy rhythm with a definite country twang, which matched the cowboy hat effortlessly.

"I used to have a law office in town, but the work got...monotonous."

Lily sensed something else behind that word, but she simply nodded so he'd go on. "So I switched things up a little. My brothers have all lived in this lodge and it was empty, so I moved up here. Closed my office and started taking on select clients."

"What kind of clients?" She'd heard through the underground about what he did. But she wanted to hear him say it.

"Women in trouble," he said unapologetically and with compassion and determination in those dark, dreamy eyes.

Lyrics sprang to her head, something she normally embraced. Slowed down her life so she could take notes.

With eyes as dark as his
A woman has no choice
But to fall.

Lily shook herself. She would not *fall* into another pair of brown eyes, no matter how chocolatey and delicious they seemed. She pushed the lyrics away, determined not to write a song inspired by this man in front of her.

"Women who need somewhere safe to stay while we work on their case," he continued. "The lodge provides an...out-of-the-way place for protection, and I still have all the resources I need here."

"Do you ever go to court? Or do you usually settle?"

Beau leaned forward, a flame in his expression now that matched the fireplace he sat beside. "I aim to settle," he said.

"And I usually do, according to my terms, in about ninety-nine percent of the cases I take."

"How long have you been doing this?" she asked.

"You'd be my fifth client," he said. "Under this type of arrangement."

"What credentials do you have to be a bodyguard?"

He blinked and leaned back into his chair, most of his face getting swallowed by the shadows cast from the brim of his hat. "I've never claimed to be a bodyguard."

"Well, that's what they call you out there."

Cocking his head, he asked, "Out where?"

She gestured in the general direction of the front door. "Out where I heard about you."

Beau let several beats of silence flow between them. Lily couldn't be sure, but he seemed to be sizing her up far too easily. Or maybe he was working through some zinging, troubling feelings of his own.

"Let's be clear," he said slowly, the rumbly quality of his voice soothing and terrifying at the same time. "If I take you on as a client, yes, you'd live here in the lodge with me. The remote location offers protection, and I suppose I manage to do so as well. We'll work on your case and get you the relief you need."

Relief. Lily wanted relief so badly, she almost sagged into the soft couch behind her.

"What's the fee?" she asked, keeping her back straight, straight, straight.

"To live here? Or to hire me?"

"Both," she said. He obviously didn't recognize her, and

she didn't need him to know she could probably buy this lodge and employ him.

"The room and board is free," he said. "You have to treat Celia, Annie, and Bree kindly, and it wouldn't kill you to help out around the house or with the horses. But it's not required."

She nodded, hoping it seemed like she actually knew how to help with horses. Her grandparents had one, but he stayed in the pasture most of the time and no one rode him.

"My fee comes when we win," he finished.

She noticed that he didn't say what it would be, and her heart thumped in a strange way, increasing when he said, "So, Miss Lily. Tell me about yourself."

THREE

BEAU COULD SEE his request made the beautiful Lily Everett squirm. She didn't physically move, but the distaste for talking about herself showed plainly in those blue eyes. She tossed her hair over her shoulder and met his eye again.

He liked that. She didn't back down from a challenge, making her vastly different from the other four women he'd helped over the past couple of years. They'd come to him with doe-like eyes and fear in every move and constant checks over their shoulders.

"I'm Lily Everett," she said again, like that should mean something to him. "I have two sisters, Rose and Violet. We're...singers."

Beau simply blinked, wondering what kind of music she sang. When she didn't continue, he said, "That's nice."

She sighed like he was being difficult on purpose, and said, "I write most of the songs, and I'm the lead singer." She shifted now, edging closer to him—or maybe toward jumping to her feet and leaving. "We've put out nine albums, and they've all gone platinum."

Beau realized what she was telling him. "Oh, I see." So she was a celebrity. Famous. And obviously in hiding, as she couldn't even email him from her normal account, or with her real name.

"What kind of music?" he asked, though he wasn't sure why he cared. If it wasn't in the realm of Garth Brooks or Chris LeDoux, he wouldn't know it.

"Mostly pop with some banjo," she said. "Violet plays."

"And you sing."

"Mm." Lily crossed her legs as an uncomfortable look paraded across her face.

"You ever been married?" Beau asked.

Lily's eyes flew to his, and he had his answer.

"He's the problem, I'm guessing." Beau wasn't guessing, but he did need Lily to feel as comfortable as possible. He wanted to help her for some inexplicable reason. Maybe the way his heart was fluttering around in his chest like it had grown wings and wanted to be set free.

Lily swallowed and cleared her throat. "He is."

"Well." Beau groaned as he stood, his muscles aching for some unknown reason. He hadn't done much that day that he didn't normally do. Exhaustion swept over him and he reached for the mantel to steady himself though it was only seven-thirty. He shouldn't be so tired so early in the evening. Maybe it was because the sun was setting earlier and earlier and with the onset of darkness by six, he was ready for bed too.

"Well," he said again. "If you let me know what else you'd

like to know, I can send you with some things. Then you can make your decision."

Lily got her to feet too, and he noticed that she was well-prepared for the weather here. It made sense, as she'd obviously been living in Jackson Hole for at least a few weeks now.

"What would you send me with?" she asked, shrugging into her coat.

"References," he said. "Past clients." Not Deirdre, but Lily didn't need to know that. He followed her to the door, getting a nice noseful of her floral scent. His pulse flapped in his neck for several reasons.

Number one, he could recognize attraction when he felt it. And number two, he absolutely was not interested in getting involved with another client. No siree, he was not.

So maybe she wouldn't hire him. He had her fake email address. Maybe they could stay in touch through that and he could ask her to dinner when she wasn't recording or traveling.

Number three, when she opened the door, they were met with falling snow. Lily froze, the word, "Oh," dropping from her mouth.

"You better hurry," he said. "Or you'll be stuck here for the night." He eyed the skiff of snow that had already started to accumulate on the sidewalk.

She faced him, that determination making a reappearance. "Can I stay here for the night?"

Beau fell back a step. "Why?"

"I didn't get a hotel in town. I was going to drive back to Jackson."

He exhaled, thinking of the long drive down the canyon in weather like this just to get to Coral Canyon. And on to Jackson? She wouldn't make it if the snow kept falling at this pace.

"I can pay for a room."

He scoffed and stepped back inside. "That won't be necessary. C'mon back in. Let me see what rooms are available." Beau honestly had no idea. Bree managed the lodge part of Whiskey Mountain Lodge, including the cooking and cleaning that came with it. Since he'd moved in a few months ago, he'd taken several guests on horseback adventures, but there wasn't anyone at the lodge on this Wednesday night.

Still, he didn't know if the rooms had been made up and were fit for a guest or not. "The guest rooms are upstairs," he said, putting his foot on the first one. "You don't have a bag or anything?"

"I can just sleep in my clothes and slip out in the morning."

"Sure, if we're not snowed in." Beau didn't turn to look at her. The odds of getting snowed in this early in October were slim, but Mother Nature had been known to dump feet of snow in these mountains whenever she dang well pleased.

He pushed open the first door he came to and found the bed made and everything seemingly in order. "This one looks available."

He knew the one at the end of the hall was Celia's, as she often stayed over in the winters or before big family events. But there were six other rooms up here.

"This is fine." Lily slipped past him, blasting him with

those lilacs or lavender or whatever flowery smell lingered in her perfume. "Thank you, Mister Whittaker."

"Oh, Beau's fine."

She flashed him a smile made of razors and closed the door between them. Beau stepped back and stared at the white-painted wood, wondering what in the world the last hour had brought him.

Possibilities, sang through his mind, and Beau cleared it quickly when he heard Lily start to sing behind the door. He thumped down the stairs in his cowboy boots, chastising himself for thinking there was any possibility for anything between him and Lily.

The very idea was laughable. She was as skittish as a baby colt with a broken leg, and he didn't have enough pieces of his heart left to go giving it to another beautiful woman.

"Help me help her if I can, though," he whispered as he entered the dimly lit kitchen and pulled open the freezer. Since he'd moved into the lodge, Celia had been keeping the mint chocolate chip ice cream in steady supply.

He pulled out the carton and scooped three large balls into a bowl. He did want to have meaning in his life, and this version of practicing law while he helped someone in desperate need had given him that. Much more than litigating divorces or dealing with trivial complaints against the city.

He wandered down the hall to his master bedroom, his ice cream bowl in his hand, and sat in the window seat to eat and watch the snow fall. He honestly wasn't sure if he wanted Lily Everett to hire him or not, and he managed to make it through all the ice cream before opening his Internet browser on his phone and typing in her name.

In less than half a second, dozens of images and articles came up, and she hadn't exaggerated her fame.

Beau exhaled, his breath fogging the cold window, and let his phone fall to his lap. He'd never handled a celebrity case before—and he wasn't sure he wanted to start now.

Maybe she won't hire you, he thought for the second time that night, but something way down deep inside him whispered that of course she would. He was the best lawyer in Wyoming, after all.

And women like Lily Everett only hired the best.

THE FOLLOWING MORNING, Beau trudged through the snow—which he actually liked—to the horse barn. Bareback didn't mind the colder temperatures either, and the black and white horse greeted him like they were old friends. Which, of course, they were.

"Hey, boy." Beau gave Bareback a handful of baby carrots, another addition to the fridge since he'd moved in. "Sun's up. This snow should be melted by noon." But Beau still wouldn't take Bareback or any of the other horses out riding. The ground would thaw into a muddy mess, and they could stay in the stables for a day or two until things dried out. Beau only hoped his soul wouldn't wither in that timeframe.

The horse continued snacking on his vegetables, not caring about Lily Everett up at the house. But Beau, it seemed, could not think about anything else. It had taken him an extraordinary amount of time to fall asleep, and even then, his dreams had been marred with dinner in a bad restaurant, with even worse music coming from the speakers.

Behind him, Black Powder puffed out his breath onto Beau's hand, and he turned. "Hey." He didn't offer this horse any carrots, because he didn't tolerate anything outside of a regular horse diet. "No riding today. I was just tellin' Bareback."

Black Powder nudged Beau's sternum in a playful gesture. Beau chuckled and ran both hands up the horse's nose to his ears. "You'll be fine. It's warm in here, and you have plenty to eat and drink."

He took a few steps away from the horses, saying, "I'll be back later, okay?" He'd need to feed them their morning rations, but he wanted to make sure Lily got out of the lodge okay.

He whistled a childhood tune as he walked back up the sidewalk toward the backdoor of the lodge. The sky was bright blue this morning, the storm having blown itself out sometime during the night.

The sun hurt it was so glinting and bright against the snow, and already the sidewalk had cleared patches as everything melted. Beau squinted against the glare and ducked inside to stomp the snow off his boots and hang his coat on the pegs in the mudroom.

He took an extra moment to breathe deeply and center himself, throw up a prayer, and run his hand through his beard in an attempt to tame it before he faced the rest of the house. He could brew coffee and scramble eggs—which was more than the rest of his brothers—but it wasn't the kitchen that called to him this morning.

Instead, he stepped toward the living room and climbed the steps. The door at the top stood open already, and he called, "Hello?" and stuck his head in.

But the room was empty. The bed made. Lily had already gone.

Like a ghost. Like she'd never been there.

Beau turned away from the huge, hollow, upper floor of the lodge, retreating quickly to the more familiar and safer level where he lived, his disappointment sharper than it should've been.

FOUR

LILY SAT IN HER CAR, her heart thumping at her to go back in and thank Beau for his time, for the accommodations she'd enjoyed last night, and for everything else he was about to do for her.

But she couldn't get herself out of the luxury SUV driver's seat for some reason. She'd scampered out the front door with her purse in tow when she'd heard whistling coming from the back of the house. As if she were a thief. Someone who shouldn't be there.

Beau obviously rose early, as the clock hadn't even ticked to seven-thirty yet, and while it hadn't been her plan to up and leave without thanking him, her feet had acted of their own accord.

"You can't just leave," she said to her partial reflection in the rearview mirror. "You don't even have his number."

But I can email him, the other half of her argued.

Lily frowned at herself, this back-and-forth new and

uncomfortable for her. She'd always known what to do, and what her life would be like. Her mother had moved with her to Nashville a year before high school graduation, and she'd sent in her song to every producer and recording studio the next week. Everything had been sort of a whirlwind since then, with five studios wanting to sign the girls, and getting the family moved, and making sure Rose and Violet finished school.

Once all the girls were adults, her parents had stepped back, and now the Everett Sisters had a manager who took care of everything for them. Shawn was the one steady person in her life, besides her sisters, and Lily often wondered how different her life would've been had she married him instead of Kent.

"It doesn't matter," she said to the windshield, her own voice sounding foreign in her ears. Because she hadn't married Shawn when she'd had the chance, and he'd moved on. Found a cute woman named Barb, and they had three tow-headed little girls now.

And she had an ex-husband who'd already gotten more than he deserved, more stress than she knew how to deal with, and almost a new lawyer to help with all of it.

She glanced at the door and heaved a sigh before getting out of the car. Imagining the doorbell to be Kent's eyeball, she pressed it hard and listened as the chimes sounded inside before lifting her finger.

Several seconds passed before Beau opened the door, and then he said, "Oh, there you are."

"Yeah," she said, a half-dozen excuses for why she was outside springing to her mind. But she didn't say any of them, because none of them were true. And she didn't want to lie to this man. "I just wanted to say thank you before I head out."

"You're welcome," he said easily, looking just as dashing and cowboy-country this morning as he had last night. Everything about Beau Whittaker indicated that he'd be easy to work with, easy to talk to, and easy to like. In fact, she already liked him.

Too much, she thought, her feet itching to flee.

"Did you want my references?" he asked.

"I don't think I need them," she said, backing up a step. "But I was wondering if I could get your phone number? Then I can check with my manager and maybe we can set up another meeting?"

Beau pulled his phone from his back pocket. "Give me your number, and I'll text you."

She recited her number as he tapped, and a moment later, her phone buzzed from inside her purse. She checked it needlessly to see he'd texted, *This is Beau.*

She looked into his handsome face and found him already smiling. She felt her own mouth curling up too, maybe for her first genuine grin in a long time. "Thanks. I'll be in touch."

"I'll be here."

Lily lifted her hand in a wave and got the heck off his porch. Relief filled her as she positioned herself behind the steering wheel again. With the sun out and the snow not that thick, she got down the canyon easily and pointed her SUV back toward Jackson Hole.

Her grandmother had understood why she'd hadn't made

the drive last night, but Lily knew she'd still have plenty of talking to do once she arrived. But for now, just as she had the previous evening, she enjoyed the silence.

She liked the way it helped her thoughts straighten. Brought new lyrics to her mind. Helped her discover who she really was and what she really wanted.

And as the miles went by under her tires, she learned she wanted to hire Beau Whittaker to help her with her current legal troubles.

And maybe, just maybe, she wanted to get to know him a little better as well.

"GRAMMA, I'M BACK." Lily entered her grandparents' house, where she'd been living for the past one year and four days. It wasn't like she needed to number the days because they were bad. But it wasn't her ideal living conditions, and everyone involved knew it—including Kent.

Though he didn't know where she was.

Yet.

That thought had her pulling her phone out to call Beau immediately. She couldn't put her grandparents in danger. She wouldn't. And she felt the circle on Kent's noose closing in on her location.

The only two people who knew where she was for certain both sat in their living room, the TV on in front of them and both of them fast asleep though the clock hadn't chimed nine times yet.

She shook her head, knowing they'd gotten up hours and

hours ago and definitely needed this mid-morning nap. So she left them snoozing in their recliners and went up the stairs to the two bedrooms on the second floor that only she'd set foot in over the past of the last decade.

Lily went through the door on the right and looked out the window. The snow hadn't hit as hard in Jackson, though there was still about half a foot in the backyard. Much like last night, she thought through what it would be like to live at the lodge full time.

Maybe the chef there could teach her how to cook. Maybe Beau would like a stained glass window over the front door. Maybe she could get on a horse and learn to ride.

There were so many maybes, Lily didn't know what to do with them all. She left her room and went back downstairs to the kitchen to make a cup of tea. She must've been too loud filling the kettle with water and setting it on the ancient stovetop, because her grandma joined her a few moments after she'd lit the flame.

"How was your meeting?" she asked, patting her curls and looking still a bit sleepy.

Lily turned from the stove and stepped into her grandma's embrace. She'd always loved her mother's parents. Loved the simple life they led on the farm. Loved the soft, powdery scent of her grandmother's papery skin.

"It was okay," she said. "You got my message about the weather?" Her grandma had a phone, but with how often she checked it, Lily didn't count it as a reliable way to communicate.

"Yes. It was really coming down. I'm glad you stayed."

Lily stepped back, a sigh leaking out of her mouth the

way air did out of a balloon. "He was...nice." Nicer than she'd
thought he'd be. Hairier too. "Wore a big old cowboy hat and
had this bushy beard." She smiled, a giggle sounding a second
later. "But his eyes...." She shook her head just thinking
about the pair of eyes Beau Whittaker had. "He could see
things," she finished. "That man doesn't miss much."

"Well." Gramma moved over to the cupboard and took
out two teacups. "That's what you want, isn't it? A lawyer
who can find a way out of the mess you're in."

That was exactly what Lily wanted. But for some reason,
she didn't want it to be Beau. She didn't want him to know
every little detail about her past. Because while he wouldn't
make a professional judgment on her, she felt certain he
most definitely would form an opinion about her personally.

And she wanted him to think the best of her.

Which is stupid, she told herself as the kettle started to
sing. She didn't know Beau Whittaker, and he didn't know
her. Even if he read through the ludicrous accusations Kent
had filed against her, he wouldn't truly know her.

No one did.

Not her greatest fans. Not her sisters, not really.

Gramma put her hand on Lily's arm and said, "Are you
all right?"

Lily looked into her grandma's watery blue eyes. She
didn't miss much either, and Lily realized she had someone
right in front of her who saw her. Who knew her. Who
loved her.

Lily shrugged. "No worse than yesterday."

"I would've thought you'd be better than yesterday."
Gramma poured the hot water over the tea bags and started

stirring her cup. Lily picked up her spoon and whisked the other cup, the fragrance of oranges and honey lifting into the air with the steam.

"Yeah, well, I don't know if he's the right one."

"Tell me about him." Gramma sat at the counter, lifted her tea cup to her lips, and took the smallest of sips. Everything Gramma did was tiny, and she ate like a bird. It would be a miracle if she drank even half the cup of tea.

But Lily would drink all of hers and maybe more. "He's different than I expected. If I'd passed him on the street, lawyer would not have been how I would've labeled him."

"No? What would you have labeled him?"

"Mountain man," she said instantly, ignoring her grandma's shocked face. "No, really, Gramma. He was Mountain Man Joe." She laughed, the sound wild and wonderful. "I almost blasted him and his brother with pepper spray. They're both so tall and so big, and they answered the door together."

"Well," Gramma said, starting her sentences with the word she usually did. "I thought you said he was the best lawyer in the state."

"He is."

"Then why wouldn't you hire him?"

Why not indeed? Lily's heart raced around like a squirrel who'd just won the acorn lottery, and she knew exactly why. But intellectually, she needed a man like Beau. *No*, she thought. She needed a *lawyer* like Beau.

The recliner in the living room squealed and the footrest clunked as her grandpa put it down. "Oh, Pops is awake." Gramma bustled around the kitchen, making another cup of tea for her husband. Pops had served in the Vietnam War, and he had a leg that still bothered him from time to time, especially if the weather went south as it had last night.

So Lily let Gramma hurry a cup of tea into the living room while she sat at the counter, thinking. Gramma returned a few moments later and set two pieces of bread in the toaster. She didn't say anything as she pulled raspberry jam out of the fridge.

Lily herself had helped make those preserves this summer, and she sensed a lecture coming as Gramma buttered the toast and put a healthy amount of jam on each slice. She had everything loaded onto a plate before she looked at Lily again.

"Well?" she said, making it seem like a question. "Why are you still sitting there? When are you going to call that lawyer and hire him?"

"I'm not sure I'm going to hire him."

"Oh, pish posh." Gramma made a scoffing sound that almost sounded like a cough. "Yes, you are. Go on and put yourself out of your misery." With that, she left Lily in the kitchen and walked into the living room with the toast.

Lily did not call Beau right away, thank you very much. She sipped her tea and stared out the window. She listened to the blinging sounds of the game show in the other room and played a game on her phone.

But her grandma was right. She was going to hire Beau, and the sooner she did, the sooner she could move into that big lodge up the canyon and get things done. Close this chapter. Make sure her grandparents were safe.

She seized onto the words wafting through her head. *One door closes and another one opens....*

Problem was, she wasn't sure which door was closing and which one was opening. She felt trapped between two worlds, with no bridge to help her get across.

FIVE

BEAU'S PHONE didn't sound on Thursday. Maybe that was because he'd put it on silent, as his mother *had* texted and called a couple of times. They set up a lunch date for the next day, and he fixed a rain gutter on the house that had become clogged with leaves during the storm, causing problems with how the water from the melting snow could drain.

But Lily didn't call, and for some reason, that bothered Beau. She hadn't taken his reference sheet, and she'd barely asked him any questions about the law or his past cases. He kept reminding himself that his previous clients in his new business hadn't either. The fact was, they knew he knew the law forward and backward. What they wanted to know was if they could stomach living under the same roof as him, large as it was.

Friday dawned with the scent of yeast and cinnamon, and Beau groaned. He loved Celia, but his mother was also coming to the lodge that day, and she'd bring something equally as delicious and calorie-laden.

So while he didn't want to, he put on his gym clothes and went downstairs to the room where several pieces of exercise equipment were kept. Bree had insisted that guests liked seeing that there was a gym at the places they stayed, but Beau had literally never seen a guest get up while on vacation and work out.

He barely wanted to do it on non-vacation days. But now that he wasn't running ten miles a minute in his law office, the beard wasn't the only thing that had changed about Beau. So he sweated through an episode of his favorite science fiction drama and went upstairs to eat the sticky monkey bread Celia was practically famous for.

"There you are," she said. "How did you sneak past me?" She set a small pitcher on the counter, and Beau peered into it. It looked somewhat like cream, but when he poked the tip of his pinky finger in it, he found it was frosting. Happiness filled him with the simplest of things. Cinnamon monkey bread and frosting this morning, apparently.

"I don't know," he said. "Maybe I've finally perfected my ninja skills."

Celia laughed and said, "Stop it." She set a couple of plates on the counter and turned to get breakfast out of the oven. "So, who was that woman who was here the other night?" So much fake casualness rode in her voice that Beau's defenses went up. And he didn't believe for a moment that Celia didn't already know.

"A potential client," he said, his mood darkening and the happiness dropping a notch. After all, Lily had made no attempt to contact him, and it had been thirty-six hours now. She didn't have any more questions, and Beau wondered if he'd hear from her at all.

"She's Lily Everett," Celia said. "Of the Everett Sisters."

Beau looked at her, and asked, "Oh, yeah? Should I know them?"

Celia scoffed and picked up a dishrag to wipe down the counter. "Of course you should know them, Beau. Their Christmas album is the one Bree plays around here like they're the only music group to ever record holiday music."

Beau tilted his head, trying to hear the Christmas tunes Bree inflicted on them starting the day after Halloween. "I guess," he said, the music escaping him.

"When is Bree going to be back?" Celia asked.

"Tuesday," Beau said, pulling off a chunk of monkey bread and popping it straight into his mouth, sans frosting. "At least that's what she told me earlier this week before she left."

"Have you heard how her mother is doing?"

"No." Sudden guilt pulled through Beau. He probably should've texted Bree to find out how things were going in Phoenix. Her parents had made the move to warmer climates about a decade ago, but her mother had taken a spill down the stairs last weekend. "I'll call her today."

Celia gave half a shrug like she didn't care what Beau did, but he knew she'd brought it up so he would call Bree. He probably should've known to do that without her prompting. Graham would've. Andrew too. Now Eli.... Eli was usually so preoccupied with something or other, he probably would've forgotten too.

Or in Beau's case, not even known it was something he should've done. Sure, Beau was great at keeping up with his clients and making sure they knew what was happening every step of the way. But he was also so very used to divorcing his feelings from whatever case he was working on. No emotion. Follow the law. Find a way to use the law to win. Prepare the argument.

None of that required him to consider how other people felt or how they were doing.

Just another reason he'd closed the law office and moved up to the lodge. He certainly didn't need the money, not since his father's death and Beau's inheritance had catapulted him to billionaire status.

But he felt like he was missing something. Maybe it was the human connection. Beau honestly wasn't sure.

"I heard your mom is coming up for lunch," Celia said next, and Beau ripped off half the monkey bread and put it on his plate.

"She is. You're welcome to stay. I think she's bringing sandwiches from Going Ham."

"That's what she said."

Celia really wasn't very good at concealing what was coming next. Beau could hear the inflections in her voice from a mile away. This time, she was trying to sound disinterested when it was very clear she wanted to stay for lunch. Had probably already put in her sandwich order for later that day.

"What's she bringing you?" he asked.

Celia's eyes flew to his, a touch of alarm in them. He

grinned at her, and she started laughing. "You think you're so smart."

"I'm not stupid," he said, chuckling along with her. "Let me guess...turkey club on sourdough." But it wasn't a guess at all. Beau had seen her eat that exact sandwich before.

When she swiped at the air and said, "Oh, you," he knew he'd gotten it right.

Hours later, after he'd gone out to the stables and finally let the horses back into the pasture, after he'd spent a healthy amount of the morning talking to Bareback, and after he'd showered, he returned to the kitchen to find his mother there with three sacks of food.

"Ma," he said, sweeping one arm around her and pulling her in for a hug. Oh, how he loved his mother. No matter what was going on in Beau's life, she'd been there, supported him, and loved him back.

After the disaster with Deirdre, she hadn't chastised him for getting involved with a client. She didn't comment about his move up the canyon other than to show up and help him clean his house in town. She ran her fingers down the side of his face now, a look of love and adoration on her face.

"How's my sweet son?" she asked with a smile.

"Doin' fine." He hadn't told her about the meeting with Lily, but he knew the whole story would be pouring from him before he finished his roast beef sandwich. "How's Tate?"

"Oh, he's fine." She started unpacking their food, and Beau recognized this tactic. She'd done the same thing with Admiral Church, and then her next boyfriend, Clint Jacobson here.

And her new man, Jason Carter, was at least a decade younger than her. Beau understood the dating pool in Coral Canyon wasn't all that big, and he just wanted his mother to be happy. Since her husband's death almost four years ago, everything had changed. All of his brothers had come home, at least for a while. They'd all found someone to love and start families with.

And somehow, Beau and his mother hadn't. He wasn't sure if she was really ready to move on, but he admired her for trying. As for Beau...well, he just wasn't sure how to pick the right woman, as all of his past relationships would suggest he was a great judge of character when it came to the courtroom, but absolutely dismal when it came to matters of the heart.

"I heard you had an exciting visitor this week," she said, shooting him a quick look.

"Not really," he said, instant annoyance springing up inside him. "I mean, a potential client came out to the lodge. I haven't heard anything more from her though." And dang, if those words didn't practically burn his throat.

At the same time, he wasn't entirely disappointed. Perhaps if she hired someone else to take care of her legal troubles, he could still be her shoulder of support through whatever lay ahead for her. He had her number; he could call her and ask her to dinner.

The thought appealed to him so much, even if it would make three giant meals in a single day.

He inwardly scoffed at his own foolishness. Surely a woman like Lily Everett wouldn't be able to drop everything in her life and go to dinner with him that night. She'd even said she needed to check with her manager. He wondered if she ran all of her personal calendar items past this manager.

"I lost you," his mom said, bringing Beau out of his head and back to the present conversation.

"I'm right here, Ma." He sat at the counter and ripped open his bag of chips. "What were you saying?"

"I asked how the new business was going." She sat beside him and sipped from her soda.

"It's...okay." He glanced at her. "I might be a bit bored. I'd like another case." If anything, then he'd have something to focus on this holiday season besides the fact that he was alone when everyone else in his family wasn't. Oh, and maybe the sting of his father's death wouldn't hit him so squarely in the chest either.

"Didn't Eli say he'd help you advertise?"

"Yeah, but Ma, this isn't something you advertise. It's a word-of-mouth thing." At least in Beau's head it was. He didn't want where he lived, or what he did, to really be out there in the world. The entire point of what he'd started doing was to keep women safe, out of reach of those who wanted to hurt them, until Beau could make sure the law was on their side and they had the protection they needed.

If he started splashing his name and face on billboards, that wouldn't be possible.

Celia entered the kitchen, and Beau exchanged a glance with his mom that indicated this particular conversation needed to be over.

"Ah, turkey club," Celia said with a smile. "How are you, Amanda?"

The two women started talking, leaving Beau to his own

thoughts. He enjoyed their company, glad he didn't have to go through another monotonous day without at least a bit of interesting conversation.

As he put the last bite of his sandwich in his mouth, his phone screen lit up. He choked at the name sitting on the device.

Lily Everett.

He made a grab for the phone, but his mother had seen it too. "Who's Lily Everett?"

Beau made a grunting noise, as his mouth was still full of roast beef and bread.

"She sings for the Everett Sisters," Celia said, and Beau's grunt turned into a growl.

"The Everett Sisters?" His mother's voice could've caused an avalanche had there been enough snow.

Beau shook his head and practically sprinted from the room, hoping he could finish chewing and swallow before he missed the call.

SIX

LILY REMOVED her phone from her ear and looked at it, a frown pulling through her whole body. Maybe Beau was out with the horses. Maybe when he went on long rides, he didn't take his cell phone.

Her line rang a moment later, and his name came up. Or maybe he just couldn't get to the phone in time.

She steeled herself and took a deep breath before answering with, "Hello?"

"Sorry," he said by way of greeting. "I saw you called?"

"Yes," she said, glad her voice didn't catch on itself. "I'm interested in hiring you, Mister Whittaker."

"Beau."

"Beau." The word did trip out of her throat then. "Do we need to meet again to go over things?"

"That would be best," he said, his own tone slipping into something more professional and less rushed than his previous words. "I'll go over everything, have the contracts for you to sign, all of it."

Lily pressed her eyes closed. "And I'll be moving to the lodge."

"Yes, ma'am," he said. "It's best if you stay here, then I can...help in any way necessary."

Help.

Lily did need help.

She'd miss her grandparents terribly, but she didn't want to put them in danger. A flash of the dark towncar that had eased down a side street near downtown Jackson yesterday crossed her mind.

It could've been anyone. Lots of celebrities came to Jackson for some rest and relaxation. Skiing in the winter. Hot springs in the summer. Shiny limos and stretch SUVs weren't that uncommon.

But somehow, as Lily had watched the shiny, not-a-spot-on-it car come to a stop and a goateed man get out, she knew he was one of Kent's guys. He looked a little greasy. A little bit like he'd do something outside the lines if he had to. A little bit sneaky.

And while she'd been wanting to call Beau and make everything official, seeing that man and that car so close to her grandparents had been what tipped her over the edge and got her fingers dialing his number.

"When's good for you?" he asked, and Lily got the distinct impression it wasn't the first time.

"Oh, uh, anytime. What works for you?"

A low chuckle came through the line, and darn it if it didn't warm her chest and make her heart purr—just a little.

"Remember how I said I don't do much but ride horses? Still true. You come on out to the lodge whenever you're ready, and I'll have everything we need." He seemed completely unruffled by her—and why wouldn't he be?

So he'd stared a little when she'd first shown up on his doorstep. That was probably from the pepper spray pointed at his eyes.

Lily pressed her eyes closed and wished she could go back in time and undo a million little things. "I'll be there in the morning if that's okay."

"Perfectly fine."

She said goodbye, and the call ended. Lily pressed the warm device to her chest, wondering if she'd ever truly feel safe again. Truly be able to relax and stop checking over her shoulder.

She'd never told Kent about her grandparents in Wyoming, but he'd somehow sniffed her out. So the best thing to do would be to disappear again. Run to the state farthest from Wyoming. Instead, she'd go an hour to Coral Canyon and then up to the lodge. Maybe hiding right under Kent's nose was the way to go.

Lily breathed, a sense of calm coming down on her like a freshly dried blanket. And she knew her move to Coral Canyon and Whiskey Mountain Lodge was an answer to a lot of prayers.

The next morning, she drove up the narrow road toward the lodge. Her to-go cup of coffee was brand new and scalding hot, from the only drive-through coffee bar in the small town of Coral Canyon. Still, it was delicious, and she was glad the options for hot, caffeinated beverages didn't disappoint just because the population wasn't very large.

Dark blue and gray clouds filled the sky, and lightning flickered up ahead, seemingly against the Teton Mountains. Lily leaned forward and peered out her window, trying to judge how close the storm was.

Too close.

At least it didn't look like snow today. Big, fat raindrops hit her windshield in the next moment, and the sound of them hit like they were made of rock instead of water. She flipped on her windshield wipers and marveled at how quickly the storm had struck.

She slowed as water began to pool on the road in front of her. So much so fast apparently caused flash floods, even up here. She was used to such things in California and Arizona, two of the nearly fifteen states she'd lived in over the course of her life.

With the windshield wipers going full speed and the rain striking the car with the beat of drums, Lily continued up and up and up the mountain. Finally, the bright yellow lights of the lodge came into view, and she pulled into the parking lot.

She parked as close as she could to the overhang, but it would still be quite the dash through the deluge of water to reach safety. The temperature indicator said it was only fifty-two degrees outside, and Lily didn't want to leave the warm, dry comfort of her car.

Thinking maybe the storm would drop its water quickly and the rain would ease up, she waited. Nothing seemed to stir from behind the windows of the lodge. No other cars were parked in the lot. For a few terrible moments, Lily felt like the only human left on Earth after some sort of cataclysmic event. Now she'd have to figure out how to survive. Now she was truly on her own.

In a lot of ways, Lily had been feeling exactly like that for much of the past twelve months. And she was ready to join the land of the living again. Live her life instead of hiding behind closed curtains and fake email addresses.

The rain did ease up, and Lily jumped from her car while she had the chance. Her purse swung against her side as she rounded the front of the car and hurried under the protection of the roof. She slowed, her heart pounding in her chest, and wiped the water from her forehead.

She pressed the doorbell and listened to the fancy chimes. Nothing moved beyond the door. She tried knocking next, but her fists fell against the huge door with little sound. Turning back to her car, she wondered what she should do. Beau knew she was coming.

Wait in the car? Call him?

The rain began pounding again, the drops actually splashing in the puddles just beyond the overhang. She was not going back to her car. She pulled her phone from her purse and dialed Beau, hoping she wasn't being too big of a nuisance.

She didn't think it too early for the cowboy, as last time she'd been here, he'd already been out to see the horses before she'd tried to sneak away. And it was almost ten-thirty after her long drive from Jackson and the crawl up the canyon in the rain.

The call went to voicemail, but Lily didn't leave a

message. A gust of wind howled around the side of the house, and Lily made a quick decision.

She opened the front door and went inside the lodge. With the door securely closed behind her, she called, "Hello? Beau?"

There were no chicken broth smells this morning. No freshly baked bread. Not even a whiff of air freshener. But the lodge felt homey and lived-in, something none of her residences had ever been.

Lily took in a deep breath, glad she felt comfortable here. After all, she was going to be living here for a while, and she didn't want to live each day with negative or awkward feelings.

She bypassed the couch where she'd sat before and went into the dining room. Beyond it stretched a massive kitchen, but there was no evidence that Beau was here or had even been here that morning. No coffee in the pot. No cereal bowl in the sink.

Dialing him again, she stood at one of the windows that looked out into the backyard, a prayer for his well-being playing through her mind.

Somewhere deeper in the house, she heard a tinny song playing. It sounded very much like someone's ringtone, and she deduced that Beau had left his phone somewhere here.

But was he okay? Maybe he'd fallen and hit his head.

Lily took a step toward the kitchen as if she'd explore this huge lodge until she found him.

Sure, she wanted to feel comfortable here, but she didn't think traipsing around the place would help. But what if he was hurt?

Torn in two directions, Lily didn't move. She didn't know what to do. And she hated feeling this way, as it was a stuck-in-place feeling she'd experienced a lot since her divorce five years earlier.

Just as she was about to start exploring—she couldn't leave the man lying in his own home unconscious—the back door opened and a man said, "Thank you, Lord." The wind whistled, and Beau grunted, and the door slammed closed before Lily could even take a step.

She was still standing like a freaking statue when he came limping around the corner, soaked from head to toe and cradling one arm against his side in a protective way.

"Hey," she said loudly, and he skidded to a stop.

"You didn't answer the door," she said, her voice wobbling a little bit. He was clearly hurt, and yet the attraction between them zipped and swooped with the power of arcing electricity. "And it was pouring buckets, so I just came in. I called you twice, but you didn't answer."

Pain crossed his face, and he continued to a barstool only a few feet from her. "It's fine. I'm glad you came in."

"What's wrong?" she asked. "You're hurt." Her hand lifted as if she'd reach out and touch him. As if such things were allowed. Or welcome.

"I was helpin' my brother round up his cattle."

That wasn't a proper explanation, but Lily didn't press for more. "Do you mind?" She stepped closer to him and managed to put her palm flat against his shoulder. Even sitting, he was almost as tall as her, and their eyes met. "I know some therapeutic touch," she said.

"Therapeutic touch?" he repeated. "What does that mean?"

"It's a bit new-age," she said, shifting her palm to the back of his shoulder and placing her other one on the front. "Oh, yeah. There it is."

"It?"

"You hurt this shoulder recently. The energy is pulsing in it." Her hands grew hot as she took on the negative energy, and she ran her hands down the front and back of his arm, throwing the energy off once she reached his hand. "Did you fall?"

"Yeah, my horse went ballistic with the thunder. I landed on that shoulder."

"Just sit still," Lily said, glad he hadn't freaked out with her declaration that she could feel his energy. "Close your eyes if you want." She moved the energy out of his shoulder and down his arm, one swipe at a time, growing warmer and warmer with each stroke.

"Let me take the jacket off," she murmured, and he helped her by shrugging out of the other side of it. He wore a pair of jeans and a black and blue striped shirt—nothing fancy—but he was easily the calmest, most handsome man she'd met in a long time.

She pressed both palms against his shoulder and then released them. "Done. I can do more later." She felt a breath away from passing out, so she dropped onto the barstool next to him and wiped her forehead again. This time, she had sweat and not rain lining her brow.

"Where'd you learn to do that?" he asked.

"Oh, it's just something I picked up somewhere," she

said. "You learn a lot when you live three hundred days on the road."

He gave her a curious look and said, "We're going to have to be honest with each other."

"I know."

"You'll give me all your cases. Not hold anything back, even if you're embarrassed."

Lily swallowed and nodded. Said, "I know," again.

Beau's rugged features softened, and he stood with a groan. "Okay, let me get some coffee started. Then we can get down to business."

SEVEN

THE LIGHTNING beyond the window caught Beau's eyes as he spooned the coffee grounds into the machine. He normally loved storms, as long as he was somewhere safe and protected. But Graham and Laney were in the final day of getting their cattle back to the ranch for the winter, and when his brother had called, Beau had gone.

No questions asked.

That was what the Whittaker brothers did for each other.

Now, if Bareback had just managed to hold on a little longer, Beau's shoulder wouldn't be aching and his pride wouldn't have taken a hit to have the beautiful Lily see him in such a state.

His jeans clung to his legs in the most uncomfortable way, and as soon as he had the coffee set to start brewing, he said, "I'm going to go change into something dry. Make yourself at home," and disappeared down the hall to his master bedroom.

He jumped in the shower and got warmed up, put on dry clothes, and returned to the kitchen, which now smelled like a more heavenly version of the lodge—with coffee.

Lily had gotten out sugar and found the cream, and she sipped from a mug that used to belong to his father. Beau stopped and stared at her, something squeezing tight in his chest and then letting go.

"Are you okay?" she asked.

He blinked and got his feet moving to the cabinet where the mugs were. "Sure, yeah. Fine."

"You said I could make myself comfortable," she said. "It wasn't hard to find things in here."

"It's not that." He kept his eyes away from hers as he poured his own cup of coffee. He added two spoonfuls of sugar and took a sip. Ah, yes, that was delicious.

"Then what?"

He might as well tell her. He had said they wouldn't keep secrets from one another. He'd just assumed it would be her that needed to reveal all, not him. He nodded to the mug she held in both of her hands. "That was my father's."

Lily looked at the mug and set it down. "I'm sorry. Does he not want others to use it?"

"He passed away, almost four years ago." Beau smiled so she wouldn't be upset. "So I doubt he cares. He's probably glad someone's using it, honestly." Because no one did. Why Graham had moved it here and kept it here, Beau didn't know.

Lily's eyes rounded. "I'm so sorry."

"It's okay, most days." Beau took another drink of his coffee. "Okay, should we go into the office? Look through a few things?"

Lily nodded, stood, and left her coffee on the counter when she followed him into the office. He settled behind his desk, his shoulder surprisingly feeling better. He knew nothing about therapeutic touch, but he could still feel the ghost of her hands on his shoulder, back, and arm.

He suppressed a shiver and pushed aside the thought that he wanted to hold her hand, touch her hair, and breathe in her perfume, and focused on the paperwork in front of him. "Okay, so this is a standard contract. It basically says you're going to hire me to represent you in any and all legal cases you now have, or that you may have in association with the current litigation." He slid the paper toward her, but she didn't even look at it.

"I think you just spoke English," she said, those blue eyes twinkling with mischief. "But maybe you better do it like you would for a five-year-old."

Beau tipped his head back and laughed. "Fair enough," he said through the chuckles. "This means I'm going to be your lawyer for all the cases you have against you now, or any new ones that come up, *if* they're related to the open ones. Once we clear those, if you get sued again, you can hire someone else."

"See, now I get that. You're going to be my lawyer." She picked up a pen and signed her name on the bottom line.

"How many cases or lawsuits are you currently facing?" he asked, slipping the paper into a folder he'd already labeled with her name.

"Five," she said. "I think."

"Criminal or civil?"

"Civil."

"The ex-husband? He is an ex, right?" He didn't want to assume anything, though he'd already checked for a diamond ring on her left hand, and Lily didn't wear one. She didn't have an indentation, nor a tan line either.

"Ex-husband, yes," she said evenly, and Beau nodded. He could deal with ex-husbands. Had dealt with a lot of them, actually.

"This gives me permission to look at your case files," he said, placing one paper near her right hand. "And this one gives me permission to look at any confidential information about you, in any court system, or any police system."

Lily didn't hesitate as she signed her name on both papers. He gathered them up and put another one in front of her. "This one I need you to fill out. It's all your personal stuff, so I can start to gather all the facts and build our case."

She filled it out, and he continued with the legal jargon until the entire packet was finished. All in all, it only took about fifteen minutes, but he felt wrung out and it wasn't even noon yet.

"Okay." He sighed as he stood. "So, when would you like to move in?" She'd signed the paperwork that said she could stay at the lodge rent-free as long as their cases were in court or unsettled and as long as she didn't disclose her location.

"Is tomorrow too soon?"

Beau turned back from the doorway. "Tomorrow?" He cocked his head. "Lily, are you safe for tonight?" His heart ached for her, for the worry that rode in her eyes, for the way she drew her shoulders up as if she were preparing for a fight.

"I'm living with my grandparents in Jackson Hole," she said. "But I have reason to believe my ex is looking for me, and is closing in. I don't want anything to happen to them."

Beau returned to his desk and with clumsy fingers because he was in such a rush, tore off a piece of notebook paper. "Write their names and address here, and I'll send the Sheriff over to make sure they're okay."

Lily looked at him with surprise. "You can do that?"

"Of course I can." He tapped the paper. "Names and address."

She wrote down the info he needed, and he picked up the paper and his phone. "Be back in a minute. You don't have to wait in here. We're done." He put in the call to Harper Sewing, the Sheriff's secretary and explained the situation.

He found Lily in the living room, curled into the recliner near the fireplace. "She said they'd do surveillance on the house for a week," he said. "Perhaps when you talk to your grandparents tonight, you can tell them to call the police if they see any suspicious activity or anyone tries to talk to them."

Lily tore her eyes from the flames in the grate and nodded. "Okay."

"I can come help you pack, if you need it." He had a feeling he'd do almost anything for Lily, and the thought terrified him to the core.

He'd felt these same soft feelings for Deirdre too, and she'd taken his heart right from his chest and spit it out.

Funny thing was, he hadn't felt anything romantic for any of his first three clients.

So why Deirdre? And why Lily now?

"I think I can handle it," she said. "I don't have much."

"No?" He thought someone like her would have a mansion stuffed to the gills with things.

"No, I just brought what I could pack in the middle of the night."

Beau held her gaze. "How long have you been living with your grandparents?"

"Just over a year."

"Where's home?"

"I have a house in California," she said. "And one in Nashville. I haven't been to either one of them in a while."

Beau nodded, wishing he could fix everything for Lily overnight. But he knew better than most how long things took. Deirdre's cases had taken up nine months of his life, and while the relationship hadn't ended the way he'd wanted, he was grateful he'd been able to help her.

And he'd be grateful for the opportunity to help Lily too.

"Okay, so you'll be back in the morning. Did you like the room you were in last night? I think we should move you farther from the stairs. Or there's the basement too." He hadn't explained all the logistics of the lodge to her yet, and Beau felt a pounding headache coming on.

Lily still hadn't said anything about her room when he blurted, "Lunch. Maybe we could talk about all of this over lunch."

"I could eat lunch."

"Great." Beau practically shot to his feet and retrieved

his keys from a hook near the garage door. "We'll take my truck." He went into the garage and she followed, whistling when she saw his vehicle.

"Wow, this is nice. This is yours?"

Beau had bought the behemoth for his birthday, a couple of months ago, only a week after Deirdre had left. "Yep," he said.

"You must be one of those lawyers who's won a couple of big cases."

Beau clicked open the locks and tapped the garage door opener. Wind and rain fought to get into the space, and he hurried around the front to open her door for her. As she squeezed by him in the small space, he said, "Nope. My dad founded the largest energy company in Wyoming. I inherited a lot of my money from him when he died."

Lily looked at him. "How much money?"

He smiled at her. "Ah, now isn't that like asking a woman how old she is?"

"You *did* ask how old I am." She settled into her seat and reached for her seatbelt.

"Only for legal purposes." He closed her door and chuckled to himself as he went back around the front of the vehicle to get behind the wheel. "Besides," he said as if they hadn't had a small break in their conversation. "You surely have plenty of money too."

"I suppose." She focused her attention out the passenger window, and Beau mourned the loss of their quick back and forth.

"My dad made all four of us brothers billionaires," Beau said, keeping his eye on the back-up camera in the dashboard. He finally looked at her and found wonder in her face. "It's what allowed me to close my practice and do what I do now."

And oh, how he loved what he did now. He felt like he had a real purpose in life instead of just trying to pay bills and practice the law he loved.

"So we can be billionaire besties," she said.

He laughed, swung the truck around so it was facing the road and said, "Oh, I don't think so. You just signed a bunch of paperwork that makes me your cowboy billionaire bodyguard."

EIGHT

COWBOY BILLIONAIRE BODYGUARD.

Lily had no idea what to do with those words. But she sure did like that he was hers. He chattered about the species of trees in the forest as they went down the canyon, then asked her if she felt like more of a bar atmosphere or more of a steakhouse vibe.

"Steakhouse," she said, not wanting to experience the Saturday lunch crowd in the only bar and grill in Coral Canyon. The steakhouse would be quieter, and she could get a booth in the corner and face away from the door.

Not that anyone here would recognize her.

They might, she thought. After all, his housekeeper had.

They sat down—yes, she positioned herself so her back was to the door—and ordered drinks before Beau said, "So Whiskey Mountain Lodge is a real, operational lodge."

Alarm yanked through Lily. "What does that mean?"

"It means we have an on-site manager who deals with the guests."

"Guests?" Lily couldn't believe she didn't know this already. And all the paperwork had been signed.

"They won't bother you," he said.

She leaned over the table, feeling fire practically spouting from her eyes. "I don't want anyone to recognize me, Beau."

"And they won't. They won't even know you're there."

Settling against the back of the booth, she folded her arms. "How do you know that?"

"They come and go all the time. No one spends much time at the lodge. There's nothing to do there. They stay when they go skiing, or they go horseback riding, or they drive down to the Tetons or up to Yellowstone."

She couldn't believe how casual he was being about this. "Where do they stay?"

"On the second floor. Sometimes we have movie night in the basement."

"Then I can't stay on the second floor or in the basement."

Beau looked up at the waitress as their drinks arrived. He grinned at her like they were old pals, and for all Lily knew, they were.

After they'd ordered their food, and she'd left, Lily said, "Is there anywhere else to stay at the lodge?" Desperation clawed its way up her throat. "My ex is very resourceful. I don't trust a guest not to see me and say something. You know, seven degrees of separation and all that. It could get back to him easily."

"Well, there's another bedroom in the family section," he

said. "I live in the master bedroom. And Bree—she's our on-site manager—lives down that hall too. There's the office, where we signed all the papers, and around the corner, there's another bedroom."

"Away from the public."

"Yes, ma'am." So maybe he'd grasped the seriousness of this situation.

"I don't like that there's an on-site manager either," she said, just so he would know. "I really can't risk Kent finding me." She hadn't said his name out loud for so long, and it felt strange and slightly acidic against her tongue. To get rid of the unpleasant taste, she lifted her soda to her mouth and drank greedily.

"Bree is aware of the discreet nature of my job," Beau said, with a bit of bite in his tone. "She's signed non-disclosure papers as well."

That fact made Lily feel slightly better. "I'll need the bedroom away from the public," she said. "I value my privacy above almost anything else."

"I understand."

She didn't think he did, but she let the subject drop.

She needed somewhere safe to stay
Somewhere to let her heart ache
And heal
And become hers again.

Lily swiped to open her phone and quickly typed in the lyrics swimming through her head, especially liking the bit about how her heart could become hers again. Her *life* could become hers again, if Beau could win these cases. She hadn't realized how much she'd been giving up when she'd said "I do."

"What are you doing there?" Beau asked, and Lily almost slammed the phone face-down on the table.

"Nothing."

Beau didn't believe her if his dubious expression said anything about how he was feeling. "All right. But you know no one can know where you're staying."

"I know," she said. "No one does. Even my sisters don't know where I've been this past year."

"Really?" Beau took another drink of his lemonade. "Tell me about your sisters."

The very idea of opening up to him had her stomach in knots, but she also realized that he was the safest person to talk to. And she really wanted to talk to him. Maybe share part of herself with another human and see how it turned out.

"First," she said. "I need to know if there are any more surprises."

"Surprises?"

"You know, secret entrances to the house. Pets I don't know about. That kind of thing."

"Well, I do have a Rottweiler."

Lily sucked in a breath. Rottweiler's were big dogs. "Oh?" she said, her voice on the squeaky side of normal. "Boy or girl?"

"Girl. Her name is Daisy. My brother took her the night you came so his daughter could draw the dog for art class."

"Daisy," Lily repeated, wondering if everything about

Beau's life would fit with hers. "My sister's names are Violet and Rose."

Beau made the floral connection immediately, as evidenced by the smile on his face. "Lily, Violet, and Rose. Seems about right."

"Rose is the youngest," she said. "She does all the arranging of our songs, as well as a large part of the instrumentals."

"What kind of instrumentals?"

Lily leaned back as her salad arrived. "You really don't know?"

"How would I know?" He shook pepper over his soup without even tasting it first.

"Well, I guess I assumed you'd look me up on the Internet."

"Ah, yes." Beau smiled and stirred crackers into his soup next. "Yeah, I don't do that." He met her eye and scooped up a bite of soup. "I prefer learning about a person right from their own mouth."

Lily watched him slide his lips around his spoon, and she'd never been jealous of an inanimate object before. Her whole body heated, and she focused on the lettuce, tomatoes, and cucumbers in front of her.

He hadn't looked her up.

He had plenty of his own money.

He was devastatingly gorgeous.

He came across as concerned and kind. Good. He was *good*.

Oh, yeah. She was in some serious trouble with this cowboy billionaire. And as their dinner progressed and she told him about her parents overseas and how Rose designed the album covers and played tambourine, Lily realized she *wanted* to be in trouble with this man.

And that was a feeling she hadn't had in a very, very long time.

IT TOOK LILY forty-five minutes to pack and load her three suitcases into the back of her car. Then all she had to do was say goodbye to her grandparents. She faced their house and tucked her hands in her pockets. This living arrangement hadn't been easy for them either. But they'd welcomed her with open arms and quick smiles and more hugs than Lily knew she'd needed.

But she had needed them. Every day, she'd needed them.

She climbed the steps and went back in through the front door. "I think that's it."

Gramma set her cross stitch aside and stood up, an anxious look on her face. "You're ready to go?"

Lily nodded, her eyes already filling with tears. She started reciting some of the Everett Sisters' most popular lyrics, even going so far as to spell them out in her mind so she could focus on something besides the emotions of this moment.

She let herself melt into her grandma's embrace and then she straightened. "I'm ready. I have to do something." She'd told her grandpa about the black town car and the call to the Sheriff's office. He said he'd watch out for anything and let the authorities know.

"I'll let you know my new number," she said. "Okay?" She stepped over to Pops and hugged him too. "Not for a week or so, okay?"

"Stay safe, Princess," he said, his voice warm and loving. "We'll be fine here." He nodded at her, and she gave Gramma one more hug before walking out of the house.

She wanted to crush her phone in her bare hand and drive out of Jackson Hole without a single attachment to it.

But she'd always be attached to this place, to her grandparents. And she wasn't stupid, which meant she wouldn't make an hour-long drive with a threatening sky above her without a cell phone. She could destroy the device in Coral Canyon and get a new one at the small electronics store in town before heading up the canyon to the lodge.

Lily had done some hard things in her life before, but getting behind the wheel of her car and driving away from the two people who had supported her the most this past year was one of the hardest.

By the time she reached the town where she'd be making her new home, she'd cried all the tears she had and shored up her store of bravery. Beau had assured her that there were no guests in the lodge for another week, and that Bree would be back on Tuesday. Until then, it was just him and her—oh, and all the horses. And a Rottweiler.

Lily needed some time to learn her way around the lodge, so she was glad she'd have a couple of days before anyone else showed up.

She pulled into the parking lot, which housed the strip of stores where the electronics shop was. Not a single car was parked there, and her hopes of getting a new phone on a Sunday in Coral Canyon vanished.

She pulled into a spot and put her car in park, feeling adrift though she had a destination. In the end, she couldn't camp out in her car until the cell phone store opened, so she continued on up to the lodge.

This time, Beau stepped onto the front porch before she could even get out of the car. "Hey," he said. "Do you go to church?"

Whatever Lily had been expecting him to ask, it wasn't that. She looked down at her black leggings and oversized sweatshirt. "Uh, not today, no."

He finished tying the tie around his neck. "My brother is coming to pick me up, but I won't go."

"You can go." Lily liked the idea of him sitting in a pew, praying.

"Nah." He loosened the tie again and pulled his phone out of his pocket. "Call Graham," he said, and the phone responded with, "Calling. Graham."

"Beau," Lily said, but he shook his head.

"Church is boring anyway." He flashed her a smile and said, "Graham, hey. I don't need a ride. Lily showed up and we're just going to stay at the lodge today."

He hung up a moment later, and Lily crossed her arms across her chest. "You didn't need to change your plans."

"It's fine." He walked toward the trunk. "You wanna pop this? I'll get you moved in."

Lily didn't want him to see that she'd reduced her life to three suitcases, but she didn't really have a choice. He was going to learn everything about her, whether she liked it or not.

So she popped the trunk and let him take in the two biggest bags. He led the way down the hall, past the kitchen, and toward the office. He rounded the corner and nodded to the first door on the right.

"That's me." He paused and turned to his left. "And that's you."

Lily looked back and forth between the two doors. There were maybe five feet separating them. Her heart twisted, twirled, and leaped, and Lily wondered if living at Whiskey Mountain Lodge was going to be a good thing or something that could break her heart.

He opened her door and went inside the bedroom. "Okay, so I'll let you get settled." He left, and Lily glanced around the room. It had a queen bed, a television, a decently sized closet, and another door that led into a bathroom. That was nice, and more than she had at her grandparents' place.

She turned in a full circle, taking in the soft colors and the peace that seemed to emanate from the walls. She leaned against the door and sighed, wondering what she'd just gotten herself into.

A hopeful feeling lifted her spirits and she pulled the door open to find Beau and ask him if she could change real quick and they could still make it to church.

He stood two feet away, as if he'd left her room and then stood in the hall, staring at the door.

"I was, uh—" He hooked his thumb over his shoulder. "I'm—"

Lily stepped forward, reached up, and touched his beard. They stood there, staring at each other, as he reached up and covered her hand with his.

Sparks fired in every cell in her body, and Lily didn't want this moment to end.

NINE

BEAU HAD no idea what he was doing. He wanted to say something before this moment broke and he could never get it back.

He wanted to convey every feeling he had, but he couldn't sort through them fast enough to make sense of them.

He was crazy, absolutely insane, and experiencing a terrifyingly insatiable craving to kiss Lily despite the odd, thumping way his heart beat in his chest, signaling that he wasn't quite ready to be kissing anyone.

"I just wanted—" His voice sounded like he'd swallowed frogs, and he cleared his throat. "I don't think you should go to church," he said. "It's pretty much the hotbed for gossip, and if you show up there, everyone will see you, and it's not safe. Or smart."

Neither was standing in this small space between their

bedrooms, her hand still cradling his face in such a tender way.

"Okay," she said

Beau pulled his hand off hers and stepped back, which caused her hand to drop back to her side too. He bumped into his bedroom door, and said, "I think I'm going to go. Unless you want me to stay and give you a tour?"

"No, go ahead," she said. Her expression and tone didn't give anything away, and he honestly had no idea if she wanted him to stay or not. He felt like if he didn't go, he'd say or do something he'd regret later.

"Okay." He took a step past her, using every ounce of self-control he had not to burst into a sprint. "I'll see you in a couple of hours then." He didn't look back or wait for her to acknowledge him. He almost ripped the door off the hinges in his haste to get out of the same space as Lily, and he drove a tad recklessly down the canyon for a couple of miles before he got his emotions in check.

"What the heck was that?" he asked himself, the burning, tingling sensation in his cheek from her touch still present. She'd started it. And all Beau knew was that he didn't want to be the one to end it.

Whatever "it" was.

BEAU SNUCK into the back of the chapel after the sermon had started, and he left early too. No reason for Graham to see him and start asking questions. He also didn't want to face his mother, or Andrew, or anyone. He probably should've put on a wig and left the cowboy hat in his truck if he wanted to stay incognito, because he was halfway home when his phone chimed.

Graham had texted with, *You came to church? What? My minivan isn't good enough for you these days?*

Beau snorted and laughed but didn't respond. He knew better than most what texting could do to a good driver, and he didn't want to end up in one of the ditches lining this canyon road.

Mom's having dinner at her place tomorrow night, Graham sent next. *She said you and Lily are both invited.*

Beau didn't think Lily would agree to that, even if it was just his family. He didn't know a whole lot about her, but she hadn't been keen on the idea of having other people at the lodge at all.

He pulled into the garage and sent a few texts to his mom and Graham, one to Andrew, and then he went inside. Celia herself wasn't present, but the smell of roast beef permeated the air, evidence that she'd been at the lodge early that morning to get the afternoon meal in the slow cooker.

Beau hung his keys on the hook by the door and called, "Lily?"

The lodge seemed to tighten up, as if it were holding its breath. No one answered him back. He wasn't sure if he should go exploring until he found her, or if he should just text her that lunch was ready and she could come eat whenever she wanted.

Maybe she'd already eaten.

He pulled out his phone and sent her the message, then got down two plates and plucked two forks from the silverware drawer. He'd just opened the slow cooker to the glorious sight of shredded beef, roasted potatoes and carrots, and au jus when the back door opened.

Dishing up some food, he asked, "You were outside?"

"It's not terribly cold," she said. "And the grounds are beautiful."

"Bree takes care of those," he said.

"Yeah, I'm learning that you don't do much around here."

His gaze flew to hers, and he found a teasing sparkle in her eyes and a cute, coy smile on her lips. "I...well, I'm busy with the horses. And work. You gave me something like fifteen hundred pages to read, I'll have you know."

He set his plate on the counter and reached for hers. "Do you like cooked carrots?"

"Absolutely not."

Beau chuckled and fished around the carrots for only potatoes and meat. He added three extra baby carrots to his plate just for good measure. "My mom used to make them with brown sugar and butter," he said as he nudged her plate closer to her and came around the counter to sit beside her. "Then my brothers and I would put tons of salt and pepper on them, since they were already so sweet."

"Hm." Lily picked up her fork. "How was church?"

"It was all right," he said. He didn't want to admit he'd barely heard two words the pastor had said. Instead, he'd replayed the drama in the hallway, wondering if he should've just leaned down and kissed her. Gotten it out of the way. Such an action certainly would've told her how he was feeling, and then he'd know if this current between them ran both ways.

She'd touched him.

He smiled as he forked up a bite of potato, carrot, and beef. "Did you go out to the stable?"

"Yes, I saw it."

"Did you go in?"

"No."

"Why not?"

"I wasn't sure if I'd get trampled or not." She glared at him for a moment, the look softening almost instantly. "But it has a great big roof on it. You should put a stained glass window in it."

Beau almost choked on his food. "A stained glass window?" He got up and grabbed a roll of paper towels from the counter. He used one to wipe his face and beard as he tried to figure out if Lily was joking or not.

She didn't seem to be. "Why would I put a stained glass window in a stable?"

"It would be pretty," she said.

Beau smiled and shook his head. "Just because I have money to spare doesn't mean I'm stupid."

Lily laughed, and Beau was glad he hadn't hurt her feelings with his statement. "I could do it, you know."

"What? Put in the stained glass window?"

"Yeah, I took a class on glass art, and we made them."

"Oh, well, let's rip down half the barn then, and you can put one in."

"Stop it." She elbowed him, still laughing, and Beau caught a glimpse of what his life could be like with this woman in it permanently.

They both sobered and ate for a few minutes. Then Beau

said, "We have a big window over the front door. Maybe you could do something with that while you're here."

"Yeah?" She looked at him with such hope, Beau realized she was worried she'd be bored in the lodge. And she might be, especially if she didn't like riding horses or reading legal documents.

"Yeah, sure."

She pushed herself off her stool. "I want to see it."

"Go right ahead." Beau almost stayed at the counter, but then he slipped off his stool too and followed her into the living room, hoping the window was as big as he remembered. "See?" he said, needlessly pointing. "It's huge. I think stained glass there would be nice."

"What would you put there?"

"Like, for a design?"

"Yeah, for a design."

Beau shrugged, already ready to get back to eating. "I have no idea." His mind worked along the lines of law and fact, not art and design.

"We could do something with your last name," she mused.

Sounded cliché to Beau, but he knew enough to keep his mouth shut.

"Or something with the lodge. Do you guys have a logo?"

"If we do, that would be Eli's realm of expertise." Beau turned back to the kitchen, waiting to gauge if Lily was ready to return too. She moved, and he led the way back to their plates.

"Who's Eli?"

"Oh, one of my older brothers," he said. "He lived here

for a while, but when he got married, he moved to California. He ran the lodge and the horseback riding stuff for a while. Big into marketing and stuff."

"So Graham's older than you too," she said.

"They're all older than me," he said. "I'm the youngest. Then Eli, then Andrew, then Graham. He's the oldest." He thought of the family dinner the following evening.

But Lily nodded, and Beau didn't want to bring up something that could shut down this peaceful feeling between them. So he let the silence be their companion as they finished eating, and then he said, "I'm going to go work on your files."

Alarm passed through her eyes, but she nodded. "Okay."

"You're welcome to sit in the office with me. Or there's a huge theater room downstairs. A hot tub. Whatever."

"I wandered around while you were gone," she said.

"Great." Beau put their plates in the sink and made for the exit. He'd barely sat down in his chair and opened his laptop when Lily entered the office too.

She held a tablet and said, "I think I'm just going to read in here."

"Okay," Beau said, trying to ignore the way his pulse skipped around in his veins like she'd just told him he'd won a gold medal.

Lily, ever a woman of the technology age, had given him a thumb drive with all of her court documents on it. Someone at the probate court had done a phenomenal job of putting everything in order, and Beau started with the file labeled *1. Kent Gulbrandsen vs. Lily Everett – alimony settlement.*

Only a few lines in, he glanced up at Lily. She stared at

something on her screen, but she didn't swipe or even seem to be reading.

"Is this alimony suit settled?"

"It was," she said, glancing at him. "He named the price, and I agreed to it. He's decided it's not enough now, and he's reopened the case for more."

Beau nodded, somewhat surprised at the audacity of her ex-husband. Re-opened alimony cases almost always got turned down, usually with a reprimand from the judge.

"He's a gambler," Lily said, pulling Beau from the records again. "So I'm not surprised he wants more money."

Beau looked into her blue eyes, ignoring the extra beat his heart put out. "Where does he like to gamble?"

"Online poker," she said with a shrug. "He went to therapy for a while when we were first married, and I'd put him on an allowance."

"How much was the allowance?"

Lily shifted in her chair. "Five hundred dollars a week."

Beau worked not to let any emotion show on his face. He didn't allow his eyebrows to lift. Didn't smile. Didn't nod.

"So two thousand dollars a month." He leaned forward and looked at the screen. "And that was the settlement, five years ago."

"Yes."

Kent had reopened the alimony, citing that inflation required that he needed more money. This case would be dismissed as soon as Beau put together a dossier about the man's gambling habit and physical ability to work. He scanned a few more lines in the brief and made a note to find out what education and skills this Kent Gulbrandsen possessed.

Because there was no way Beau would allow Lily to give him another cent.

Hours later, Beau's head hurt and his eyes felt like they would never be able to focus on small print again.

The blue light from the computer screen made him cringe, and he leaned away from the desk and stretched his arms high above his head.

His phone chimed, and he practically lunged for it. "Graham's bringing Daisy back," he said. "You up for meeting my dog?"

Lily wore a hint of trepidation in her gaze, but she set her tablet on the desk and stood. "I'm ready. Might as well get it over with."

"She's sweet," he said.

"How much does she weigh?"

"Daisy?"

"No, you, cowboy." She shook her head. "Yes, the dog."

"Probably seventy pounds or so. She's sweet as pie, honest," he said. "Graham has a baby at home and everything. Daisy loves Ronnie."

That seemed to pacify her, and he waved her through the doorway first. They'd just arrived in the living room when the front door opened.

Daisy barked, her paws scrambling on the tile, trying to get a grip, as she launched herself toward Beau. He laughed and caught sight of Graham and Laney walking through the door next.

Then Daisy reached him, giving him sloppy, slobbery

kisses that required all of his attention and strength to keep the animal from knocking him down completely.

Even as preoccupied as he was, he was very aware of Laney saying, "Oh my goodness, it *is* you. Lily Everett."

Beau looked up to find Laney pressing one palm to her throat as the other hand fluttered around excitedly. "*The* Lily Everett."

"Oh, uh...."

Beau shot forward, and positioned himself between Lily and Laney. "She's my client," he said, quite emphatically. Probably a bit possessively too.

Graham looked back and forth between his wife and his brother, and at last tried to get a glance at Lily, concealed behind Beau.

"Graham," Beau said. "This is a *client*."

"It's okay," Lily said from behind him, and he twisted toward her. "I'll wait in the office." She spun and retraced her steps back to the hall, disappearing before Beau could fully breathe again.

"Graham," he said, turning back to his brother.

"I'm sorry," Laney said. "Celia said she'd put a roast on, and your mom took the kids home." She glanced at Graham and slipped her hand into his. "We thought we'd spend the afternoon with you. But it's fine, we'll—"

"It's okay," Beau said.

Several moments passed, and finally Graham broke the silence by asking, "You sure she's just your client, bro?"

TEN

LILY STOOD JUST OUT of sight, listening to Beau talk to his family. She sucked in a breath when Graham asked Beau if she was just his client.

She held it while Beau let the silence go on and on. And she wanted to stab something into her ears when he said, "Of course that's all she is. I'm not making that mistake again."

Lily moved then, not wanting to hear any more of this conversation. But Beau's words reverberated through her head. *I'm not making that mistake again.*

So he'd had a client-slash-girlfriend before. And obviously, that hadn't ended well.

Lily made it to her bedroom and closed the door behind her. Her heart beat furiously fast for some reason she couldn't name, and she pressed her hand over it, the same way Laney had been doing.

The lodge had great sound-proofing, as she didn't hear another noise. Not a voice. A footstep. Nothing.

She sank to the floor and drew her knees to her chest. It wasn't cold in the lodge, but she felt an iciness in her chest where her heart should've been.

Which was completely ridiculous. She'd met Beau less than a week ago, and just because she may have been fantasizing about holding his hand and tracing her fingers through his beard just before he kissed her didn't mean that would ever be her reality.

She wasn't even sure she wanted that reality. That meant trusting another man. Giving some part of herself she'd reclaimed and determined never to lose again.

About fifteen minutes later, a soft knock came at her door, and she jumped away from it.

"Lily?" Beau's voice sounded muted through the wood. "You okay?"

She wanted to ignore him. She could claim she'd fallen into bed and taken a nap. But when the handle started to drop, she leapt toward the door and opened it.

"Hey," she said, lifting her eyes to his. She would not let him see that she'd somehow turned into a marshmallow since meeting him, and that he possessed the flame that could melt her.

"Sorry about that." He looked nervous, like he'd been caught eating cookies before dinner. "They're gone."

"They could've stayed," she said. "They're your family." Her throat closed after the last word, and she thought about the last time she'd seen her sisters. Fourteen months ago, and they'd both told her to take the time she needed to sort things out.

Rose had said the music would still be there once Lily

was ready, and Vi had insisted she could keep their producers happy with her solo album in the meantime.

That album still hadn't come out, but Vi kept Lily up to date through regular emails.

"Doesn't matter," he said. "My obligation is to you, and...yeah."

Lily crossed her arms, her hip automatically cocking too. "So that's what I am. An obligation." She practically spat the last word from between her lips.

Beau blinked, her animosity obviously punching him in the face. "I—"

"Who was the client you dated?" she asked, feeling reckless and out of control.

He backed up a step. "Excuse me?"

"I heard you tell your brother I was just a client, and that you didn't want to make the mistake of dating a client again."

She heaved in a breath, but the air in the lodge had run out of oxygen.

"Well, I—I—" Beau sputtered. He finally found his words and said, "Did you want to be my client?"

"Yes."

He studied her, those eyes that missed nothing looking and finding what he wanted to know. "And...did you want to...?" The touch of hope in his expression spurring Lily down this path of crazy she'd started on.

She couldn't get the words to line up, so she just reached out and slipped her hand into his. He squeezed, and all the tension between them faded away.

"You wanna go see the horses?" he asked.

All Lily could do was nod.

✳

THE NEXT WEEK passed in a repetition of days. She always found Beau in the office in the morning, reading on the computer and making notes in that notebook she really wanted to take a peek at.

She'd pad down the hall to make coffee and then join him in the office. About mid-morning, they went out to the stables. He fed the horses while instructing her in small jobs she could do, like cutting twine on bales of hay and moving the hose from one trough to another.

The weather turned nasty, and guests showed up at the lodge for the weekend, and Lily met Bree.

The woman who ran the lodge was cute, with almost black hair that was very curly and hung just below her shoulders. She had a quick smile, and Lily envied her for that.

Lily didn't feel like she could truly be friends with anyone, because she didn't trust them. But she introduced herself to Bree, using her real name, and Bree hadn't even blinked.

So at least Lily had found somewhere that the Everett Sisters hadn't reached yet. She made a mental note to tell Vi, so she could tell Shawn, and he could figure out how to sell more records in Wyoming.

In the afternoon, Beau would slip his hand into hers and lead her outside. They walked down the hill toward the ranch at the bottom, where his brother and sister-in-law lived, and he mostly told stories about his childhood in Coral Canyon.

She'd opened up and told him a few things about herself

and her sisters. But she felt like he was already getting an unobstructed view into her life with every paragraph he read, so she kept the conversations easy and light.

Another Sunday came, and he stayed home from church while Bree went down the canyon with Celia. The forecast had snow in it for that evening, so when he shouldered on a coat and said, "I'm going out to the barn for a bit," Lily wasn't surprised.

She'd lived through a winter in Jackson Hole, so she had plenty of warm clothing.

"Wait for me?" she asked. "I can help."

"Sure."

She put on wool socks and stuffed her feet in her designer boots. She already wore her fur-lined leggings, and she grabbed her scarf before heading back to the mudroom for her coat and gloves.

"Aren't you cute?" Beau leaned against the wall and watched her approach.

They'd never really talked about what they were doing out at the lodge—besides the legal work, obviously.

Lily actually liked the non-label. She just knew she just didn't want to be a *client* or a *mistake*.

But did she want to be his girlfriend?

"Thanks," she said, tipping up onto one toe and doing a little spin. "But, seriously, it's supposed to snow soon, and we need to get your precious horses ready." She grinned at him, glad when he helped her put her coat on and then kept his arm around her.

Lily still wasn't entirely sure she knew what she was doing, but she felt a measure of happiness walking down the sidewalk with Beau that she hadn't experienced in a long time.

"So how did you meet Kent?" Beau asked, startling Lily out of her bubble of joy.

"Oh." She blew out her breath. She'd anticipated him asking her some questions about her adult life, and she searched for how she felt about sharing specific things with him.

"You don't have to tell me."

She tightened her arm around his waist as she felt him drifting away from her. "I will. I want to."

But she took several steps before she said, "Kent was a very charming man. He was a bartender when I met him."

"Oh," Beau said, his voice full of surprise. "I wasn't expecting that."

"Yeah, he worked in a sports bar in Las Vegas, and he could bet on the games while he served drinks." Lily gave a mirthless laugh and shook her head. "Apparently, I thought that was charming."

"How old were you when you met him?"

"Twenty-six," she said. "We got married four years later. That lasted five years." She couldn't believe she'd given almost a decade of her life—nine of her best years—to Kent.

"The initial divorce seemed amicable," he said, his voice a touch too light to be casual.

"It was," she said. "He asked for things, and I gave him everything he asked for." A hint of bitterness crept into her voice, but she didn't care. She was allowed to be bitter that some of her hard earned money and fame went to Kent every month.

"He didn't work while we were married. He lived in my house in California, and racked up bills on who-knows-what."

Beau opened the door to the stable, and she stepped through first. The scent of hay and horses met her nose, and Lily actually liked it. She never would've pegged herself as someone who wanted to be around unpredictable animals and all the smells they made, but Beau's horses brought Lily a sense of comfort she'd been missing in her life.

"I think I probably know," Beau said, bringing the door closed behind him and making the light dimmer. "But what happened?"

"It was the infidelity that finally pushed me over the edge," she said, turning to face him. "And his complete unwillingness to stop or go to counseling." She shrugged, though the reason for her divorce still stung pretty deeply. "I want to say that I tried, you know?"

Beau nodded and reached up to cradle her face. "Yeah, I know."

"Have you ever been married?"

"No, ma'am."

"Oh, don't start with the ma'am stuff." She swatted at him, and the tender moment between them evaporated. "Just because I'm six years older than you doesn't mean I'm ancient."

Beau laughed, the sound booming and wonderful and filling the rafters of the barn. Lily joined him, leaning into him until he put his arms around her. They sobered together, and he brushed her hair off the side of her face again.

"I like you," he said, his voice dipping into the husky range.

A bolt of fear hit her, but she managed to stay still and in his arms. "I like you too, Beau." She smiled up at him and he leaned down and pressed his lips to her forehead.

A wonderful spray of stars spread from where his mouth had been, and she kept smiling as he wrapped his arms all the way around her and held her close to his heartbeat.

DAISY WOKE LILY the next day, but she stayed in bed and listened to the dog bark and bark and bark. Beau's voice joined the fray, and he didn't sound happy about the early morning wake-up call.

But Lily didn't mind. She'd lived most of her life backward, with late nights and waking after noon. But in the year she'd taken off from her music career, she'd learned about the simple things like watching the sun rise and lying in bed for a few moments while the night gave way to day.

She loved soft moments like these, and she took several minutes to enjoy them. Then she reached over to her nightstand and picked up her phone. She'd been using a new email address every week to contact her sisters and let them know she was okay. She hadn't given them any details about where she was, and she kept her messages short and with generic happenings like shopping or eating lunch with a friend that could happen in any city in any country.

So she hadn't told them about the horses, or Daisy, and definitely not about Beau. But this morning, as she thumbed out a new email for her sisters, she felt the loss of them way down in her soul. The three of them had spent so much time together over the years, and Lily hated that Kent had taken Vi and Rose from her too.

But all of that was about to change. She had a lawyer now, and he was going to help her get rid of Kent forever. She told all of that to her sisters and paused, wondering if she should mention that she'd started dating a man.

Too soon, she thought and sent the email without any indication that her life had changed all that much.

As she let the phone fall to her chest, she acknowledged that it had changed a lot. New place to live. New lawyer.

New boyfriend.

A smile curved her mouth, and Lily closed her eyes and fantasized about what it would be like to kiss a man like Beau Whittaker.

Sudden trepidation ran through her, because she hadn't kissed a man in a very, very long time. And Beau was the kind of man who was the best at everything he did.

ELEVEN

BEAU SAID, "THANK YOU, CHARLIE," and hung up the phone. He burst into a standing position, a huge smile on his face. But Lily wasn't in the office to celebrate with him.

They'd settled into a routine fairly early, and Beau knew he'd find her in the kitchen with Celia.

Lily had been at the lodge for about three weeks now, and she'd started getting cooking lessons from Celia every day that the older woman worked at the lodge.

She'd settled down around Graham and Laney, and had even met their kids without a problem. He often found her and Bree chatting, curled up in the couch with mugs of hot chocolate, too.

He entered the kitchen, his excitement over the news he'd just gotten close to exploding out of him. But the scent of sugar and butter and baking pie dough reminded him how Thanksgiving was only a few weeks away.

Celia leaned both of her forearms onto the counter and

flipped a page in her cookbook. "Yep, here it is," she said. "And yes, we need the buttermilk."

Lily straightened from the fridge, a carton of the liquid in her hand. She caught sight of Beau, and he saw the slight fumble in her step.

"Great news," he said, his own grin stretching his face so wide he felt like a clown.

"Yeah?" Lily set the buttermilk on the counter next to Celia. "What kind of news?"

"The judge threw out the alimony suit."

Lily squealed and rushed around the counter, laughing as she came. He caught her around the waist and twirled her, but in the tight space, her foot hit one of the legs of the barstool.

"That's great," she said, pure joy on her face. Beau wanted to solve all of her problems, and euphoria filled him as she put both hands on his shoulders and looked up at him.

"One down," he said, brushing her hair back, the thought of kissing her pressing forward in his mind until he couldn't think of anything else.

Celia cleared her throat, and Beau realized he'd started to lean down toward Lily as if he'd kiss her with an audience present.

Foolishness raced through him, and they jumped apart as if Celia was their mother. She wore a fond look on her face, her eyes deep and knowing.

Beau ducked his head, wishing he had his cowboy hat on so he could hide his eyes. "Anyway, I'm done for today. I'm going to go riding."

"All right." Lily moved back around the counter and

joined Celia on the other side. "Celia's teaching me how to make coconut cream pie and pecan pie."

"For Thanksgiving," Celia said. "And your mother is coming out to the lodge tonight for dinner, remember?"

Beau did remember, and he nodded. "She's bringing Jason?"

"Yes, sir."

"And what about you?" he asked.

Celia turned away from him, her voice straying into the higher range when she asked, "What about me?"

Beau leaned against the counter, enjoying himself maybe a little too much. But Celia had teased him plenty over the last few weeks, and she could take some of her own medicine.

"Oh, come on, Miss Celia. I heard the ladies at church talking about you goin' out with someone." Beau had been going to church with Graham, same as always. Lily stayed home to keep the risk of someone knowing about her presence at Whiskey Mountain Lodge as low as possible.

He hadn't heard even a whisper about her, and he was satisfied that she'd been able to move in and feel comfortable without a single person in Coral Canyon knowing about it.

Celia did all the shopping for them, or Bree added a few items Lily needed when she went into town to supply the lodge.

Beau had gotten her a new phone and told the clerk it was to keep in the stables. Boy, he'd gotten a puzzled look for that, but in the end, Roy had simply said, "Must be nice to have so much money you can buy a cell phone for a horse."

"Thirteen horses," Beau clarified, a smile stuck to his face as he paid and left with the new device.

"I have no idea what you're talking about."

"Okay. Guess I'll ask Agnes Duffin."

Celia spun around, her eyes flashing. "You will do no such thing."

Beau knew Celia and Agnes hadn't seen eye-to-eye on the Halloween carnival years ago, and he simply widened his grin. "Maybe you should invite your boyfriend up for dinner too."

"It's...." Celia exchanged a look with Lily, who shrugged.

"Might as well tell him. Beau has a way of figuring things out just by looking."

Beau stared at her, wondering if that were really true. She thought he didn't have to work to figure things out? Though he felt he could read people decently well, he definitely did some investigative work in order to get the results he wanted.

After all, he'd seen the name assigned to the alimony case, and it had only taken two phone calls and one Internet search to know that Judge Tomlinson had a history of ruling in favor of shorter alimony periods if the party requesting the money was unemployed.

And Kent happened to be unemployed, something Beau put as their first counter against increasing the payments or lengthening the time Lily had to pay.

"You know about her boyfriend?" he asked Lily.

"Women talk while they cook," Celia said, stepping around the counter and planting her palm against Beau's chest. "You go ride your horses."

"What's his name?" Beau fell back a step though he could've easily resisted the pressure against his chest.

"None of your business," she said. "It's not serious enough for me to be talking about him like he's my boyfriend. When it is, I'll let you know."

Beau chuckled and shook his head, finally moving toward the mud room of his own volition. "Fine," he said. "But for the record, I think it's great you're seeing someone."

His mother had been back in the dating scene for about a year too, and Andrew had struggled with it the most. He seemed to have come around now, though, which made family get-togethers less awkward.

He ducked out of the house and was greeted by the whipping wind and the threat of rain. He glanced up into the sky and whispered, "Thank you for sending me Lily Everett," as he continued toward the stables.

THANKSGIVING APPROACHED, and Beau worked tirelessly on Lily's cases. He'd submitted three more rebuttals and all they could do now was wait.

It seemed he was doing a lot of that lately. Waiting for the first snow. Waiting for the responses form clerks and paralegals and courts that he needed. Waiting for the pie to finish cooling.

Waiting to kiss Lily.

Something powerful existed between them, and Beau was enjoying it. But he also had almost a sixth sense about her, and he could tell she was not ready to take their relationship out of the hand-holding category.

Honestly, he wasn't sure if he was ready either. So he spent a lot of time waiting, and thinking, and analyzing—and not just court cases.

"Movie night," Lily proclaimed one morning when she brought in his cup of coffee.

He looked up from his laptop. "What?" He accepted the coffee from her and took a sip. It was too hot and too bitter, but he didn't say anything. He kept sugar packets in his top drawer, and when she wasn't looking, he'd pour in a couple.

She had been getting better in the kitchen, but he'd learned she simply liked her coffee more bitter than he did.

"Movie night." She sat across from him, her pale blue eyes watching his. "You said you'd go get pizza and we'd watch something in the theater room with Andrew and Becca."

"Did I?"

"Beau." She shook her head, a smile touching her mouth for a moment. "I like all the meats with pineapple on my pizza."

"I know," he said. "You've told me like a thousand times."

"I have not."

"Yes, you have." He went back to his computer screen. "Movie night on Friday. Remember how you're getting pizza on Friday? I want to watch Out to Sea on Friday."

He glanced up and grinned at her. "I haven't forgotten."

Lily sighed, her smile fully forming and looking a little soft around the edges. "I guess I'm just excited to see some new people," she said.

"You don't like people." Beau leaned back in his chair and studied her.

"I like people just fine," she said. "I just don't trust them not to tell their aunt that they met me. And then their aunt puts it on Facebook, and then the next thing I know, Kent is standing on the doorstep."

Beau started nodding halfway through her explanation. "I get it. Becca says she has something for you to sign, but that she's willing to say she got the autograph at one of your signings overseas."

Lily nodded, her lips pressing into a tight line. "She's texted me a bunch of times. She seems nice."

"There's no one nicer than Becca," Beau agreed. And yet Lily still looked a little nervous.

"So I'll get the pizza at seven and we'll start the movie at eight."

"That's the plan." She stood, having stopped hanging out in the office with him while he worked. She might go do something with Bree, or whip up scrambled eggs and bacon for breakfast, and a few times, Beau had caught her out in the stables.

She still didn't want to ride, but she did seem to like the horses. She'd also measured the front window and ordered all the supplies she needed to transform it into a stained glass masterpiece she would not allow him to see.

"My metal work will be here tomorrow," she said as if reading his mind. "And then I can start on the window."

"I can't wait to see it." He grinned up at her, and she beamed down at him, and Beau wondered if he could lunge to his feet and kiss her right now.

But he didn't want their first kiss to be a quick, fumbling affair. He wanted to take his time with her, not make sudden moves.

"There's peach delight for breakfast," she said.

Beau's stomach growled and his mouth watered. "I'll be right in. I just need to finish this email."

"All right." She let her fingers trail along his and then she walked out. Beau watched her go, wondering if maybe, just maybe, he could kiss her that night during the movie.

Don't be stupid, he warned himself. His brother would be there, and Andrew was far less subtle than Graham. Sure, he could spin any tale for the newspapers, but sometimes he just told things how they were too.

"Maybe after the movie," Beau muttered to himself. "After everyone goes home except you and Lily."

With that possibility in his mind, he went back to the boring, monotonous work of trying to find a case where a spouse didn't get half of the assets in a divorce.

TWELVE

LILY SPENT a few hours outside every day, her only relief from the walls of the lodge. Yes, they were beautiful walls, with great art hanging on them. Gorgeous hardwood floors. Wonderful company when Celia was there, and even when she wasn't Lily enjoyed talking with Bree and just hanging out with Beau.

But she had not left the property in almost five weeks, and something gnawed at her from the inside out.

Beau left often—every week for church, and at least once or twice on other days of the week. Tonight, he'd get to go get pizza, see that there was a world beyond Whiskey Mountain Lodge, the stables, and the towering Teton Mountains in the distance.

Lily had taken a liking to a butter-colored horse named Dandelion, and she took the reins Beau had taught her how to put around the animal's neck and said, "Come on, girl."

She could bridle her now by herself, and she just took her out to the pasture that ran along the back of the property.

Dandelion seemed to like it back there, especially if Lily brought her hay and oats.

Lily liked the way the horse followed her, her head down, as if she trusted Lily not to lead her into anything dangerous.

She liked that the horse stayed nearby her, even in the pasture, as if Lily somehow comforted the horse, when it was really the other way around. She liked talking to Dandelion about her sisters, and the songs Rose was working on, or the conversations Vi had with their manager. She even liked hearing about their parents and what they were up to in the Middle East.

She loved this slower pace of life, but a twinge of sadness for her old life still radiated through her.

She led Dandelion through the gate and into the pasture before dropping her reins. "Go on and eat."

The horse did, picking through the dried and dead grasses for the hay she hadn't gotten yesterday.

The sky looked threatening today, and Lily knew she'd have to cut her time in the pasture shorter than normal. She tossed the oats she'd loaded into her pockets on the ground and sighed as she stepped over to the fence and put her foot on the bottom rung.

"I miss singing," she said to the wind, the sky, and Dandelion.

Her songwriting ability hadn't left her, but she'd stopped writing down the lyrics that came to her. She honestly wasn't sure she'd be able to pick up where she'd left off. Maybe such a thing wasn't possible, no matter how much her sisters or her manager reassured her that it was.

Because she was a different person than the one that had written the songs on the previous albums. And what if people didn't like the person she'd become?

The metamorphosis would show in her songs. It always did for the truly great songwriters.

She opened her mouth and sang something she'd written a decade earlier, before she'd even met Kent. It was one of the Everett Sisters' biggest hits, and Lily still loved it now as much as she had while writing and recording the song.

He blows into town like a blizzard
Whistling and wearing that smile
Does he see me standing in the aisle
Will he still be here come spring?

She stopped after the first verse and collected the reins again. She'd barely reached the stable when it started snowing, and by the time she finished brushing down Dandelion and putting the equipment back on the hooks just the way Beau had showed her, she had to walk back to the lodge in a snowstorm.

It was only a few minutes, though it was uphill, and she pulled her coat tighter around her. Beau would be happy for the snow, proclaiming winter to be one of his favorite seasons. How that could be true, Lily didn't know. He simply hadn't been to California or Miami or Cancun. If he had, he wouldn't want to live in brown, dead, and now snowy Wyoming.

It did possess a beauty of its own though, and Lily paused to appreciate it. There was something magical, something moving, about the way bare branches held the snow and transformed into works of art.

Snowflakes landed on her lashes, and Lily giggled as she tipped her head back and tried to catch them in her mouth. She spun for a moment and then stopped as she stumbled down the hill a little bit, the winter wonderland around her almost too good to be true. She felt peaceful here, and the thought of putting on concerts in twenty-eight cities over the course of three hundred days made her stomach turn.

Maybe she didn't want the singing life anymore. At least not the one she'd had before.

"Thank you for letting me be here," she said aloud, not all that great at praying. But Beau and Celia and Bree all prayed before every meal, and she'd felt things settle in her life in a way they never had before.

Their faith was something quite new to her, but she was learning to lean on it. Borrow it a little when she needed to. And develop her own.

Her phone rang, bringing her back to the present, and she startled. No one called her. Her pulse picked up as she fished the phone out of her pocket with her mittened fingers.

It was Beau, and her adrenaline and panic subsided as she answered.

"Where are you?" he asked.

"On my way back to the lodge from the stables," she said. "I had Dandelion in the pasture, but I got her back before it started to snow."

"Yeah, I saw her in the barn."

Lily turned around as if she'd see Beau coming up behind her. She couldn't see more than two feet in any direction.

"I don't think you're on the sidewalk," he said next. "I just walked down there and back, and I didn't see you."

Panic built in Lily's stomach, surging upward and choking her. "I'm...."

"Which way were you going?"

"Up to the house," she managed to push past her vocal chords. She caught a glimpse of yellow light to her left, and she started walking in that direction.

"Stay where you are," he said next. "The last thing I need is you wandering in any direction so I can't find you."

"Beau," she said, her voice tinny and desperate even to her own ears.

"You can't have gone that far," he said. "I'm getting the spotlight. Just wait for me."

"Don't hang up," she said as she stopped walking.

"Tell me what you see," he said, his voice her only lifeline at the moment. If she were being honest, *he* had been her anchor, support, and lifeline for a long time now.

"I can't see anything," she said.

"Did you go past the pool?"

"I don't think so. I didn't see it."

"Did you see a swing set?"

"No." She'd been out to the playground with Bree as they got everything ready for winter one day a couple of weeks ago. It was way past the house, beyond the pool, and almost on the edge of the property.

"Were you going uphill or downhill?"

Lily tried to remember. "The house is uphill."

"But did *you* go uphill or downhill?"

She thought of the spinning and catching the flakes on her tongue. She'd definitely almost fallen *down* the hill.

"Downhill," she said, embarrassment filling her. She'd been walking in the wrong direction. How had that happened? Had she really gotten so turned around from a few snowflakes?

They fell fast and furious now, fat flakes that completely obliterated the landscape.

"Okay," he said. "I'm going to text Graham, and one of us will find you, okay?"

Tears gathered in Lily's eyes. She couldn't even see somewhere to sit down and wait. Find shelter. Could they really find her standing out in the middle of nothing?

"Lily," Beau barked. "Okay? Don't move."

"Okay," she said, hating this weak feeling inside her and hoping that Beau found her before his brother did.

"Okay," he said, the tension in his voice still present. "I'm going to turn on all the lights on the outside of the house. Tell me if you can see them."

She turned in a slow circle, her desperation growing when she realized how dark it was and that no, she couldn't see any lights.

"I'm sorry, Beau," she said, catching the sob before it left her throat. "I can't see them."

"Can you turn the flashlight on your phone and hold it up?"

"Yes, just a sec." She put the call on speaker so she could still hear him and swiped and tapped until her flashlight came on.

She tried to stay in a tight radius as she turned in a slow circle, shining the light out in front of her as she did. Lily had never seen darkness approach so quickly, but it seemed to go from light to dark in a matter of moments. The wind blew the snow sideways, sometimes whipping it right into her face and making her hair heavy with water.

"Please find me," she whispered. Each moment felt like it took a week to pass, and surely Beau could move faster than he was. She banished the thoughts and took a deep breath. She was the one who'd gotten herself lost when the walk from the stable to the lodge was a straight shot.

"Hey, maybe you can sing," he said through the phone, startling her. She'd forgotten he was there, and she hoped he hadn't heard her desperate plea for him to find her.

"Sing?" she repeated.

"It should carry pretty far in this weather," he said. "Snow muffles everything else, and your voice could really cut through." He puffed and huffed, clearly marching through the storm like a champ.

Like her boyfriend.

Like her bodyguard.

He was going to rescue her, and she hadn't even known she'd need help with this part of her life.

She took in another breath, the cold sinking into her skin and making her shiver. When she started singing, her voice felt a bit rusty, but she soon found her groove. She sang a ballad she'd written the year after the divorce was final, and it was sad and full of emotion. Though she hadn't been particularly devastated about the ending of her marriage, there were still feelings of sadness and loss, as if the last five years had meant nothing.

"I can hear you," Beau said. His breathing quickened, like maybe he was running. "I see your light. I'm almost there, sweetheart. Almost there."

She heard Beau's footsteps only a moment before the dark figure of his body broke through the snow. She cut off her voice at the same time he swept her into his arms, and more relief than Lily had ever known washed over her.

He held her tight, and she gripped his shoulders, the warmth of his body and the safety of his arms feeling very much like she'd made it home.

THIRTEEN

BEAU'S HEART thumped and pumped in his chest like he'd just run a marathon. Of course, hiking through a storm, searching for something he couldn't see, really got the adrenaline flowing.

Thank you, he thought as he smoothed back her wet hair. *Thank you for leading me to her.* He pressed his lips to her forehead and said, "Let's get back." He secured his hand in hers and ended the open call he had with her so he could call Graham.

"Hey," he said when his brother answered. "I found her. We're about halfway between the cabin and the stable. We're headed back to the lodge."

"Good news," Graham said, and he sounded truly relieved. "I'll head in then."

"Thank you, Graham." Beau didn't think the words could possibly convey how grateful Beau was that he could call his brother, and Graham would rush outside almost immediately.

Beau kept his eye on the compass on his phone, and he got them back to the lodge as quickly as possible. Lily was shivering and soaking wet by the time they burst through the backdoor into the mud room.

"Found her," he called, and Celia and Bree appeared in the doorway, anxiety evident in their expressions.

"I've got hot coffee," Celia said, ducking back around the corner and into the kitchen.

"I'll go start her shower." Bree dashed off the other way.

Beau started peeling the soaked, semi-frozen layers of clothing off of Lily. She'd been out there longer than she realized, but Beau understood what this kind of snow could do to a person if they didn't get warmed up quickly.

"Come on," he said when he got down to her base layer. He tugged her toward the hallway, as she hadn't moved or spoken yet. Shock.

"Coffee," Celia said, thrusting a cup at Lily. She took it with trembling hands, and Beau helped her steady it as she drank.

"You're going to get in the warm shower," he said. "Stay in until you feel normal. Bree will have it on pretty cold at first so you can warm up gradually."

Lily looked at him then, a bit more life in her face already. "I'm fine."

"You are not fine. You're cold and in shock. I'm going to have Bree stay in your room until you get out, just to make sure you're okay." He arrived at her door and knocked to let Bree know.

She pulled open the door a moment later, flashed a look at Beau, and took Lily by the hand. "Come on, hon. Let's get you good as new."

Beau stood on the threshold of the room, watching helplessly. But Lily was in good hands, and she was safe now. It would have to be enough, because they couldn't get down the canyon to the hospital tonight anyway.

He pushed out his breath and went back to the kitchen, where Celia had a hot cup of coffee for him too.

"I can pull some frozen meatloaf out," she said, worry still riding in her eyes. A rush of affection for the woman hit Beau, and he gave her a grateful smile.

"That would be great, thanks."

She put her arm around him, and Beau leaned into her like he could steal some of her motherly comfort. "You'll still have your movie night, okay? Just no pizza, and no Andrew and Becca."

Beau started nodding his head. "Yeah. Maybe."

"No maybe about it. I've gotten to know Lily pretty well." Celia moved away and opened the freezer. She rummaged around and pulled out a gallon-sized zipper bag with two foil-wrapped packages in it.

"These take an hour to heat up, and then you two will be snuggling downstairs, that romantic comedy she picked out playing on the screen." She tapped on the stove, something beeped, and she opened a cupboard to find a baking sheet.

Beau just watched her, a bit numb himself. When he realized his jeans were wet, and that he indeed needed to change or be cold for the rest of the night, he stood and said, "I'll be right back."

"All right," Celia said, still busy in the kitchen.

Beau escaped to his bedroom, a heavy dose of exhaustion hitting him right behind the lungs. Breathing wasn't particularly easy, but he managed to pull in some air and push it out. Suck in, push out.

He'd been working long hours on Lily's cases, and there hadn't been any threat to her from Kent, not that Beau had known about. He'd emailed all of his law enforcement contacts within a hundred mile radius, and none of them had seen the man.

But somehow, Beau ended up playing the rescuer anyway, albeit he hadn't considered the snow to be Lily's biggest enemy. A sigh washed through his body, and he stripped off his wet clothes. After a quick shower in the hottest water he could stand, he wrapped a towel around his waist and stood in front of the mirror.

"Maybe it's time to trim the beard," he muttered to himself as he ran his hand along his jaw. It hadn't taken him all that long to grow the facial hair, and he supposed he did look a bit on the mountain man side of things.

In the end, he didn't want to take the time to shave right then, so he got dressed in warm, comfortable clothes—a pair of sweats and a T-shirt—and went back to the kitchen. Lily sat on the same stool he'd vacated a few minutes ago and their eyes met as he entered.

"Hey, there," he said, his voice soft and filled with all kinds of telling emotions. He cut a glance at Celia, but she didn't even look at him. "How are you feeling?"

"So much better." Lily had both hands wrapped around a

huge mug, with marshmallows bobbing near the rim. "Are we still up for a movie?"

"Of course." The clock indicated that their planned date with his brother wouldn't have started for another hour, but Lily stood like she wanted to go downstairs right now.

"I'll call you when the food is ready," Celia said, finally turning toward Beau and smiling. "You two go on."

So Beau did. He went on down the stairs ahead of Lily, turning on lights and wishing he'd thought to come down and switch on the space heaters too. The basement of the lodge could get quite chilly in the winter, but Andrew had made sure to put a heater in every room.

Beau bent to twist the knob on the one in the living room, saying, "There's some blankets in the closet in the theater room. Sorry it's so cold."

Lily's hand touched his then, and all the nerves and worries and fears partying in Beau's chest simply disappeared. He looked at her again, noting the coolness of her skin against his, which felt feverish to him.

"Thank you," she said, something intense burning in her gaze. "I don't know what I'd have done without you. Probably still be wandering out there in that storm."

Beau pushed her damp hair over her shoulder, wishing he could confess all the soft things he felt for her. "Well, you're not," he said instead. "And Celia said you have a movie already picked out?"

Lily seemed to relax, and a smile drifted across that mouth that was driving Beau toward the brink of madness. "Yeah, come on. I think you'll really like it."

He didn't mention that he already knew it was a romantic

comedy, and that he didn't particularly enjoy those. He thought he'd probably enjoy anything if he could do it with Lily. She handed him the case for the movie, and he pointed to the closet. "Blankets in there."

After putting the disc in the player, he gathered all the remotes and faced the rows of recliners facing the big screen. "Do you want to sit in the back or the front?"

"Right there." She pointed to the back row, which had two loveseats side-by-side. His heart beat at triple time, and he followed her to the one all cozy in the corner.

She sat first, and he joined her, thrilled when she spread the blanket over both of them. He got the movie playing before lifting his arm around her shoulders. She snuggled into him as if she really liked him, and Beau's blood ran a little faster in his veins.

He couldn't help thinking about Deirdre and how she'd done all of these things too. Maybe not here at the lodge. But she'd definitely acted as if she'd liked him. She held his hand, and spent hours talking to him late into the night, and kissed him while the snow fell outside.

The similarities of the relationship ran through Beau's mind, and the fear and doubts he'd had kept streaming through him as the movie played. Lily giggled, clearly paying attention the screen, but Beau hadn't comprehended a single thing.

"Lily," he whispered, deciding he had to do something to get his heart to stop racing and his mind to stop circling around things he didn't know.

"Yeah?"

"You like me, right?"

She lifted herself up and looked at him, her eyes illuminated by the bright lights from the movie screen. "Of course, I do, Beau."

He swallowed, his mouth suddenly so dry. "My last client...her name was Deirdre. I thought she liked me too."

Lily sat all the way up, the movie clearly forgotten. "Go on."

"Turned out, she didn't. I mean, not really. Not as much as I liked her." Beau had no idea what he was saying. "I mean, I'm not saying you need to like me as much as I like you, but I'm just wondering where you see this...us...going." He gazed at her, determined to be strong and straightforward. Lily seemed to appreciate that more than beating around the bush.

"I honestly don't know, Beau."

He nodded, his worst fears manifesting themselves in those words. "I live here," he said. "This is what I do. I know you travel and sing and tour...." As he spoke, he realized how hopeless a relationship with her was. And how big of a fool he'd been, falling for his client *again*.

At least he hadn't kissed her yet. At least he wasn't all the way in love with her. Yet.

Beau looked away, watched what was happening on the screen though it didn't make sense to him. Not a whole lot did at the moment.

"I shouldn't have—" he started, but as Lily traced her fingers up his arm to his face, his voice went mute.

"If I do ever get married again," she said, her voice soft and absolutely piercing. "I'd want it to be with someone like you."

Beau wasn't exactly sure what that meant, but he did know that all of his fears fled with her words. And when she leaned toward him, closing her eyes as she neared, Beau's heart and desire began firing like cannons.

The first touch of her mouth against his happened while his eyes were still halfway open, and as he realized that she'd kissed him, he brought his hands to her face and kissed her right on back.

And suddenly, things between them did make sense. No, not everything was worked out and planned for and ready to go.

But it didn't matter. As he continued to kiss Lily, all the shouting voices in his head were silent. They had nothing to say, and everything felt absolutely right.

FOURTEEN

LILY WASN'T sure what she would do when her cases were settled, when it was time to leave Whiskey Mountain Lodge —leave Beau.

But it didn't matter right then. With the flickering light from the movie playing on the back of her eyelids, and the spicy scent of Beau's cologne in her nose, and the way his face seemed to fit in her hand, she didn't want to be anywhere but with him, in this theater room, kissing.

He finally pulled away, leaving Lily breathless and wondering if she should've kissed him weeks ago. She sucked in a breath as he gave a low chuckle and said, "Well, I guess we don't have to have everything figured out right now."

She tucked herself back into his side and stared at the screen. "No, probably not."

"You will be honest with me, though, right?" He pressed his lips to the top of her head. "Just tell me how you feel, okay? I'd rather know than wake up one day and find your bedroom empty."

She shifted against him, turning her head to see his face. "Is that what Deirdre did, Beau?"

"Yeah, pretty much." The sadness emanating from him made Lily wonder if he was even over his other client yet. "And she got a new phone, and I couldn't reach her. When I finally tracked her down—I mean, I'm not a stalker, but I have ways of finding people—she said she just wanted to return to her 'normal life' in Colorado."

Lily didn't know what to say. "I'm sorry," she tried, but it didn't sound quite adequate enough. "How long ago was that?"

"Last Christmas. Just after the New Year, we got all her cases settled, and she disappeared in the middle of the night."

Almost a year, Lily thought. It seemed like enough time for him to be in another relationship, but she was still getting to know Beau Whittaker. She'd liked everything she'd seen from him, right down to how he marked his documents with blue post-it notes so she'd know where to read and then sign.

She liked this lodge, and the country way of life. It was slow, and steady, and peaceful, in a world where Lily had never experienced slow, steady, or peaceful. Her life had been one of glitz and glam, private drivers and all-nighters.

He kissed her again when the movie ended, and they went upstairs together to find the kitchen lights dim and the meatloaf sitting on the stovetop. Celia had left a note that she didn't want to bother them, and that she was upstairs if they needed anything.

Beau gazed at the note, and Lily said, "How do you know Celia?"

"My brother hired her," he said. "Years ago. She's been cooking here for almost four years, for all of us actually, as we've all lived in this lodge for a time."

"Are you going to stay here forever?" she asked.

Beau looked thoughtful for a moment, and then nodded. "Yeah. I sold my house in town. Gave up my practice. I think this is home for me now." He glanced around. "I do love the lodge."

Lily did too, but she kept the words beneath her tongue. "Do you like renting it out?"

"It's not so bad," he said. "The guests don't bother me. Bree takes care of all of that, and we have a part-time house-keeper too. Her name's Annie."

"I like Bree. And Celia."

Beau's grip on her hand tightened. "I'm glad. I don't think I'm hungry." He released her hand and started opening drawers until he found the aluminum foil. Then he wrapped up the cool meatloaves and put them in a gallon-sized bag. "Don't tell Celia, okay?" He gave her a sly grin, and she smiled back.

"Oh, you can't keep anything from her," Lily said. "But nice try."

Beau laughed, and Lily joined in as they went down the hall toward their bedrooms. He paused outside his door, slid his hand up her arm, and grinned at her. "Pretty good ending to the day, though, right?"

"Definitely."

Beau leaned down and kissed her again, really taking his time to let her know that he liked her. Lily liked him too, and by the time he slipped through his door and closed it, she wasn't even sure she knew how to walk.

ON THANKSGIVING DAY, Lily woke to an alarm so she could get to work on the pies before the turkey needed to go into the oven.

Celia had been teaching her the ins and outs of dough and fillings for a couple weeks, and Lily had agreed to make a pecan pie, as well as a pumpkin one. She wasn't too fond of the last one, but it needed to bake the longest, so she flipped on the lights in the kitchen and got out all the ingredients she needed.

She'd given Beau a list, and he'd gone into town yesterday, barely making it back with his life, if he was to be believed. He'd claimed the grocery store was a madhouse, and Lily had enjoyed listening to him tell the story as well as use those big muscles to bring in loads and loads of groceries.

She lined up all the spices, cans, and other ingredients she needed and focused. She couldn't be thinking about Beau, and Beau's muscles, and kissing Beau when she needed to concentrate on a recipe to make sure everything got incorporated in the right order.

She started with the dough, which needed to chill while she made the filling. She measured and mixed, molded and formed, before sliding the pie tins into the oven.

"Well, look at you," Celia said as she bustled into the kitchen. She moved right over to the stovetop, where two perfectly browned pie crusts cooled.

"Morning." Lily finished drying her hands and scraped her hair into a ponytail. "I'll have the pumpkin in the oven in a few minutes. It'll be yours by nine, I promise."

"These look great, Lily." Celia gave her the kind of motherly smile Lily craved, and she basked in the compliment.

"Thanks."

Celia opened the fridge and started pulling things out. Vegetables, and stock, and butter. She was making the stuffing, and then she'd get everything ready for the turkey too. Apparently, Beau's mother was bringing rolls, and Graham and Laney were bringing yams, while Andrew and Becca were supplying all the drinks.

A river of nerves poured through Lily as she added the eggs to her pumpkin mixture and got it ready to pour into the crust. She'd met Graham several times, and Laney once. Andrew and his wife had never made it to the lodge after that storm, and Beau's mother, who he said visited often, had not come out once either.

She was supposed to, but something had come up. So this meal they'd be sharing at two o'clock this afternoon would be the first time she met a lot of the people in Beau's family. She wasn't sure what he'd told them about her, and she wanted to ask him about it so she could be prepared.

Instead, she plowed through making the pecan pie, adding it to the oven with forty-five minutes left on the timer for the pumpkin pie. She checked the clock and saw she was going to make her nine o'clock deadline for being out of the oven by at least thirty minutes.

"I'll be right back." She left Celia in the kitchen, slicing celery, and headed down the hall to the office. Surely Beau would do a little bit of work even though it was a holiday. He started every day in the office, seven days a week.

But he wasn't there when she poked her head inside. His laptop sat closed, and she turned away from the office. After facing his door, she stalled. She wasn't going to go in there, and she didn't even want to knock that badly.

He'd come out soon enough, so she went back to the kitchen and asked Celia, "What do you need me to do?"

"Can you grab that bread we cubed yesterday? I put it in the garage."

"Sure, yeah." Lily went down the hall the opposite way this time and pulled open the door to the garage. Something clanged as metal hit cement, and Beau muttered something under his breath.

"There you are," she said. "Celia said the bread for the stuffing was out here."

Beau looked up from under the hood of a car she hadn't seen before. Lily was once again reminded that Beau had a life beyond this lodge, while she did not. "Bread?" He stepped away from the car and reached for a blue mechanic's rag.

He approached her, looking handsome and rugged with the beard and cowboy hat he normally wore, along with all that grease on his hands. Lily licked her lips, and said, "We're making Thanksgiving dinner while you play around out here, I'll have you know."

Beau simply laughed, wiped his hands, and came up the stairs to take her into his arms. "I'm not playing around. I'm trying to make this car run."

"Why?" Lily held onto his upper arms, enjoying the adrenaline rush flowing through her veins. "You have that SUV, and it works great."

"Yeah, but this is a Corvette," he said. "Come see." But he never got to the car, instead taking advantage of the privacy of the garage to kiss her.

She kissed him back but jerked away when she heard the squeak of the garage door.

"Can't find it?" Celia asked, and Lily ducked her head as if her face would show what she and Beau had been doing.

"Um," she said.

"It's over on the deep freezer." Celia pointed toward the front far corner, and Lily got her feet moving in that direction.

"And Beau, your phone keeps going off." Celia turned and went back into the house, leaving Lily and Beau alone in the garage again. Lily collected the tray of bread cubes and started to head back into the house.

Beau preceded her and held the door while she squeezed past with the tray. She veered into the kitchen while he continued on to the office. She continued to work with Celia, and the whole lodge filled with the delicious smells of Thanksgiving. Pumpkin pie, roasted turkey, and butter, as Celia put more of the dairy product in the vat of mashed potatoes she made than Lily had ever seen.

She never saw Beau again, and then the front door opened, and a woman called, "Hello?" startling Lily.

"Who's that?" she hissed as Celia tossed a towel onto the counter.

"That's Beau's mother," she said. "Amanda."

In the next moment, a beautiful woman entered the kitchen carrying a few bags of rolls in her hand. A man came behind her, also bringing in more bread.

And that was when Lily realized this would not be a simple meal.

FIFTEEN

BEAU STEWED IN HIS OFFICE, though he knew his mother and her boyfriend had arrived. He couldn't tell Lily about the phone call from the Sheriff in Jackson Hole, not on Thanksgiving.

He'd seen Kent the previous evening, but by the time he'd gotten home, it was too late to call Beau.

Sheriff Glamp hadn't seemed too concerned about Kent, and apparently he'd only been in town for a day or two. Perhaps he was visiting the area for the holidays. The Sheriff said he'd keep an eye on things and see if he could question Kent to know the true intent of his presence in Jackson Hole.

But Beau knew the reason. Kent had somehow tracked Lily to the area, and it was only a matter of time before he came to Coral Canyon.

His heart beat heavily beneath his ribs, and Beau turned

toward his laptop to try to figure a few things out just as his mother appeared in his doorway. "Hey, baby."

"Mom." Beau remembered it was Thanksgiving, and he was about to have a lodge-full of company for dinner. Not only that, but Lily would be meeting most of them for the first time. It was *not* the first time he'd had a client at a holiday meal, and his family was great.

More noise came down the hall, indicating someone else had arrived. By the sound of things, it was Graham and Laney and their kids.

He gave his mother a hug, and said, "Did you bring Jason?"

"Yes, he's currently sampling the turkey to make sure it's edible." She laughed and pulled away. "I met Lily. She seems nice."

"She is nice," he said, wondering if he should treat Lily like the girlfriend she was or if he should pretend they had a purely professional relationship. They hadn't had a chance to discuss any of that, so he went into the kitchen blindly.

Sure enough, Graham and Laney were both there, laughing with Celia about something. Lily stood off to the side, a smile stuck to her face in an odd way, and Beau made a beeline for her. "Did you meet everyone?"

"Sort of," she said.

Beau turned back to the crowd, wondering if he should make a big announcement or just let her meet people more organically.

Andrew chose that moment to arrive, so Beau kept his mouth shut. Becca put down several bottles of sparkling cider, and she and Andrew came right over to Beau.

"Hey," Andrew said. "We need to reschedule that movie night." He cut a glance at Lily, his public relations smile in place. "I'm Andrew, Beau's brother."

Lily shook his hand, her grin becoming a bit more authentic. "Lily Everett."

"This is my wife, Becca." Andrew slung his arm around Becca, and Beau marveled at how far they'd come in such a short time. He knew Andrew's path to the perfect romance hadn't been easy, but still. He'd managed to complete it. Beau couldn't seem to be able to take those final steps, with any of the women he'd dated over the years.

"All right," Celia said in a loud voice. "It's time to eat."

Every eye fell on Beau, and he realized with a start that he was the man of Whiskey Mountain Lodge this year. He stepped away from Lily and said, "Welcome, everyone." He glanced around. "Graham, did—?"

"Bailey put the place cards on the table," Graham said.

Beau looked at it, somewhat surprised to find it perfectly laid out and ready for the meal. Celia really was a miracle worker.

"Right. So we'll say grace, and then you can find your place at the table. Celia will tell us about the food, and Andrew, will you say the prayer?"

"Sure thing," his brother said, folding his arms.

Beau swiped his cowboy hat from his head, adding his own mental plea to the Lord to keep Kent away from Coral Canyon and Lily until he could figure out what to do to Andrew's vocalized prayer.

"Okay, so food is all here," Celia said as soon as the group had said, "Amen," together. "There's plenty, so don't be shy.

Lily made the pies, and we'll serve those with coffee in a couple of hours."

All eyes flew to Lily, even Beau's, but she seemed to take the extra attention fairly well. Before he could step away, she sidled up to him and touched his arm lightly. "Can we sit by each other?"

"Depends on where the cards are," he said, watching as people walked over to the table, checked the spot, and picked up the plate there.

"They can't be moved?"

Beau looked at her, realizing she was genuinely concerned about the seating arrangements. "We don't normally move them, no." He wanted to take her hand, squeeze it, comfort her. "But it's a small group. I won't be too far away."

She drew in a deep breath, said, "Okay," and walked away from him. He watched her go, the news that Kent was only a short hour away screaming through his mind.

You're not telling her today, he told himself. She deserved a stress-free Thanksgiving. He followed her, and once everyone had loaded their plate with turkey, mashed potatoes, yams, and creamed corn, he said, "All right. Time for our gratitude share. Who wants to go first?"

"I will," Jason said, surprising Beau. All eyes turned to him, and Beau caught the look of complete terror on Lily's face from where she sat two places down from him. He hadn't prepared her for this meal, and regret washed over him.

"I'm grateful to be here with your family," Jason said with shining blue eyes. "It's been a while for me since I've had this opportunity."

Beau nodded, glad the man hadn't said anything sappy about his mother. From there, the gratitude statements just went around, and when it was Lily's turn, she said, "I'm glad to be eating a traditional Thanksgiving dinner this year."

Everyone accepted her answer, but it made Beau wonder where she'd been last year. And the year before that. Or before that. Was she with her sisters or her grandparents? Or eating on the road with her crew?

All too soon, it was Beau's turn to talk, and he hadn't prepared anything. "Oh, um." He put his fork down and glanced down the table. "This year, I'm grateful for this lodge and that it brings us all together."

The last couple of people finished and the eating commenced. He kept an eye on Lily, but she didn't seem to have a problem talking to his mother or Celia, who had thankfully been seated beside her.

He thought he did a pretty great job of hosting the meal and once everyone had eaten, he went downstairs with his brothers to play pool.

"So," Graham said. "You and Lily are getting serious?"

"Are we?" Beau asked, shooting a look at Andrew. He hadn't specifically told either of them he was dating Lily, though he supposed they could assume anything they wanted.

"That's what I'm asking." Graham lined up his shot and hit the ball squarely into the corner pocket.

"Oh, I don't know," Beau said lightly, feeling very out of his element with playing pool and having this conversation. "She's a celebrity, you know? She's not going to stay in Coral Canyon."

Andrew took the cue from Beau, who obviously wasn't going to use it, and said, "Are you dating?"

"A little," Beau hedged. He certainly wasn't one to kiss and tell, and none of the brothers had ever done that. "I like her." But he wondered if he'd like any pretty woman who came to him for help.

He reminded himself that he hadn't felt anything romantic for his first three clients. Not until Deirdre had he mixed his business with his personal life. "So what do we think about Jason?"

"Man's had it rough," Andrew said, making his shot. "Wife died over a decade ago. Only son never comes to visit."

"I like 'im," Graham said. "He's a hard worker, and he seems to like Mom."

Beau nodded, watched his brothers shoot pool and talk about their lives, but his thoughts never drifted too far from Lily—or Kent.

His skin itched to get back upstairs, back to the computer, back to the cases. He'd gotten three of them settled or dismissed already, but the last two were coming together much slower. Things had been so easy, so casual, at the lodge that he hadn't realized he was in a race against time.

He kicked himself for letting his focus slip from the cases he needed to win to the woman he needed to win them for.

"Pie," Lily called down the steps, and Beau shot to his feet, earning him a look from Graham.

"What?" Beau asked. "She made the pies and I want to be supportive. Celia's been teaching her how to cook."

"Oh, boy," Graham said, racking his cue stick. "And we're going to eat these pies?"

"Be nice," Beau said as he started for the stairs.

"Of course I'm going to be nice," Graham said. "She's your *girlfriend*."

"Shut up," Beau hissed as they reached the top of the steps. But Graham and Andrew laughed, which got him a worried look from Lily.

"Which do you want?" she asked, her pie server held at the ready.

"Both," he said. "And do we have—ah, yes. Ice cream. I want that too." He grinned at her and then Celia as they served the pie, and he went to sit in the front room to eat his. It was quiet and with every sugary delicious bite of Thanksgiving pie, Beau prayed for a solution to the cases he still had before him. Prayed for Lily's continued safety at the lodge. Prayed to know what to do about their relationship.

God didn't seem to be in too big of a hurry to answer him though. Maybe He was off eating pie too.

SIXTEEN

LILY LOVED BEAU'S FAMILY. They felt like the kind of people she could spend weekends and holidays with for years to come. Becca reminded her of her youngest sister, Rose, and Lily fought the urge to call her sisters and wish them a Happy Thanksgiving.

Sure, they emailed, but Lily hadn't physically spoken to one of her sisters in so, so long. What would it hurt? How would Kent even know? She'd been through at least a half a dozen phones and numbers over the course of the last fourteen months.

But they haven't been, a voice whispered in her head, and she lifted another slice of pecan pie out of the tin for the cutest little blonde girl—Bailey, Graham and Laney's daughter.

True, Kent could've bugged her sister's phones, but would he still be listening all this time later? It wasn't something she could risk, and she finished serving the pie and stepped back from the counter.

Celia manned the huge barrel of ice cream, and Lily asked for a bowl of that. "No pie?" Celia asked.

"You know, because I made it, I'm not feeling like eating it." Lily wasn't sure why. Several people who'd already finished eating had told her how good the pies were. But Celia didn't ask any other questions, almost like she understood what Lily meant, filled her bowl with ice cream, and let Lily escape the kitchen.

She just needed a few minutes to herself. Some down time. Some silence.

She found it in her bedroom, behind the closed door, and propped up in bed. The ice cream was cold and creamy, sugary and oh-so-satisfying. Since she'd already eaten about twice as much as her stomach normally held, she only made it halfway through the bowl before she simply couldn't stuff another bite down.

Leaning back against the headboard, Lily closed her eyes, her mind drifting through the memories of the day. She felt warm and cozy, safer than she'd ever felt. She loved this lodge, and Wyoming, and the horses out in the stable.

Did she want to go back to her old life once her cases were settled? Beau had basically asked her that question—at least he'd hinted at it—and Lily hadn't quite known how to answer. Her sisters and manager were expecting her back. It had always been her intent to get things cleared with Kent and then return to her song-writing and singing career. But was that what she really wanted?

HER COWBOY BILLIONAIRE BODYGUARD   133

She honestly didn't know, and that was almost as hard as trying to take another bite of ice cream.

A knock sounded on her door, and she knew it was Beau. How, she wasn't sure, but she said, "It's open," and the door swung in.

Sure enough, Beau followed it, coming all the way inside and closing the door behind him. Lily's red alerts all went off. He'd never done this before, and the anxious look on his face was new too.

She scooted to the edge of the bed and stood up. "What's wrong?"

"Okay, look, I know it's Thanksgiving—"

"Beau, what's wrong?"

"The Sheriff in Jackson Hole called this morning and said he's seen Kent around town."

Lily sucked in a breath, her emotions spiraling all over the place. She wanted to say something, but her brain was having a hard time putting together a coherent thought and sending it to her mouth.

"It's fine," Beau said, reaching out with both hands and sliding up from her elbow to her shoulder. "He's going to keep an eye on the hotel, and maybe he's just in town for the holiday. It could be a pure coincidence."

Lily shook her head. "No, Beau. If Kent is in town, he knows I have family there."

"He's got officers at your grandparent's house." He leaned down a little and peered at her. "You don't need to go to Jackson Hole. There's nothing you can do there."

She seized onto that thought, as it had been the one she was trying to form. She twitched, like she knew where her car keys were, but she hadn't driven in such a long time, she actually didn't.

"I just wanted you to know. This is why you hired me, so that you'd have eyes and ears on things you can't control. He doesn't know you're here, and even if he did, this is private property."

Lily folded herself into Beau's chest, his arms coming easily around her. She wondered if she'd embrace him like this if he were simply her lawyer. Were his other clients as relieved and grateful as she was?

She put the thoughts out of her mind. It didn't matter what his other clients did. She was his client *and* his girl-friend, and if she wanted to stand in the circle of his arms and take comfort from him, she could.

"Okay," he said a moment later, his voice soft and husky. "I have to go back out there." He eased her away from him, pressed his mouth to hers for a brief moment, and then ducked back out the doorway.

Lily didn't know what to do with her mixed up thoughts and feelings. She crossed the room to the window to check on the weather, wondering if she could go down to the stables and spill her secrets to the horses.

The sky held a shade of gray that wasn't all that unusual for November in Wyoming, but it wasn't raining or snowing. She could bundle up and make sure she was back well before the sun started to set.

She collected her bowl of nearly melted ice cream and headed back to the kitchen. It held cheery yellow light, and people sitting at the dining room table with cards in front of them. They chatted, they laughed, and they were everything Lily wanted in a family.

After putting her bowl in the sink, she ducked right back out before someone could grab her and invite her to come sit down too. She put her feet in her boots, zipped up her coat, wrapped her scarf around her neck, and searched her pockets for her gloves.

Ready, she checked her back pocket for her phone and then set off for the stables. The horses seemed to look up in unison, and she smiled at them. No, she didn't necessarily want to ride one, but she did like coming to visit them.

"Hey, guys," she said to them, feeling the slightest bit foolish for talking to animals who couldn't speak back to her. But she didn't do it in the presence of others, and sometimes she just needed to get her feelings out.

She stepped over to the nearest horse, a gray and white quarter horse she couldn't remember the name of. She stroked her hand down his nose, and said, "Happy Thanksgiving." She moved down the row of stalls, saying hello to the horses and getting handfuls of oats from a bag hanging by the door for each one of them.

When she finally went back to Dandelion, she said, "Well, Kent's come to Jackson Hole." The worry she had for her grandparents tripled, and a sense of helplessness felt like it was about to crush her.

"I just don't know what to do." But she had done something—the best thing she knew how to do. She'd hired Beau. He'd already settled three of the cases, and he had people watching out for the people she loved. For her.

But she still felt like she needed to do something. "I

should probably go," she whispered to Dandelion. "Just get in my car and drive until I run out of gas."

The horse didn't indicate if that was a good idea or a bad one, but nosed her face further into Lily's palm, searching for a stray bit of oat.

Lily wasn't really going to get in her car and start down the highway. But she honestly didn't know if she could stay here and do nothing. Could she call her grandmother? Would Kent have somehow put a trace on their line?

She wasn't sure, and that was the most upsetting. With a man like Kent, anything was possible, while at the same time, she knew he didn't have any money. So who could he hire to sneak into a home where the two people who lived there never left at the same time? How could he afford fancy tracking software or private investigators?

He couldn't. If he could, he wouldn't be coming after her for more money, or an extension on the alimony, which was set to expire in another year. Beau had gotten that case thrown out, and now he just had to work on the royalty situation. He'd told Lily that judges very rarely granted anything extra outside the original divorce decree, and that Kent certainly wasn't entitled to a lifetime of support because they'd been married for five years while she was a singer before and after that relationship.

Lily unconsciously pulled her phone from her back pocket, toying with the idea of making a call. She'd spent so long cut off from the outside world, and the urge to speak to someone from her former life rose up, choking her.

She tapped in her grandmother's number and listened to the line ring. It was still a landline, so her number wouldn't show on a screen or anything. It would be a miracle if someone answered, but the line only rang twice before her grandma said, "Hello?"

"Gramma," Lily practically breathed. "It's me. Don't say my name," she tacked onto the end.

"Oh, hello," Gramma said, her voice full of joy. "Stu it's...Rose."

"Rose?" Pops practically yelled. "What's Rose doin' calling?"

"Happy Thanksgiving," Lily said, tears pricking her eyes. "You guys are okay?"

"Just fine, Dear," Gramma said. "And you? Did you get some turkey?"

"Lots of turkey." Lily half-sobbed and half-laughed. "And mashed potatoes, and yams, and bread. Wow, this family knows how to pack away the bread." Lily had eaten a few rolls herself, simply not able to get enough of them.

"What about you two? Did you go to the church dinner?"

"Sure did," Pops bellowed, and Lily yanked the phone away from her ear. He must've picked up the line in the kitchen, and while she didn't like talking to both of them at the same time, it was good to hear his voice too.

Neither of them seemed afraid or worried about anything.

"We had ham and turkey," Pops continued. "I had both, and then the pastor's wife brought out that layered chocolate cake I like."

Lily smiled at the horses, thinking about her grandparents eating with a few others who didn't have family for the holidays. Making their own family.

"Well, I just wanted to say hello," she said, her voice catching. "Let you know I'm okay."

"That's good," Gramma said. "We're so glad you called. We love you."

"Yes," Pops said. "Love you, Princess."

"Stu," Gramma said sharply, and Lily said, "Okay, I have to go," and hung up. She squeezed the plastic case on her phone as the familiar desperation returned. Pops had just called her Princess. Would Kent know that was his nickname for her, not Rose?

Had she just put them in more danger?

SEVENTEEN

BEAU NOTED the moment Lily slipped out the back door. He stayed at the dining room table and kept half of his attention on the game of Hearts in front of him. But his laughter died much quicker, and he didn't engage in a few conversations the way he should have.

He probably shouldn't have told her about Kent today. She'd been shocked and scared, as Beau had gotten quite good at reading her emotions as they played across her face. He wasn't even sure when he'd decided to tell her. Perhaps when he'd returned to the kitchen for more pie and Celia had told him that Lily had taken a bowl of ice cream down the hall to her room.

She did like her private time, and Beau had tried to give it to her whenever she needed it. His soul screamed at him to get out to the stables and make sure Lily was all right. His brain told him to get down the hall and back to work on the two cases that still needed his attention.

He had to have missed something. Maybe there was a line, a sentence, a loophole he needed to take advantage of to get these items off Lily's plate so she could be free again.

Free.

Once she was free of Kent and her past, what would her future be like? Would she stay here?

Beau's mind whispered all kinds of things, and he missed playing a winning card that could've won him the trick he needed. Frustrated, he threw down his cards as if this game actually meant something to him. But he didn't care about Hearts. He needed to figure things out with Lily. So many things.

"I'm out," he said as Andrew started shuffling the deck again.

"Come on," his brother said. "Just because you're not winning." He grinned at Beau, and Beau remembered the carefree days when he did win most games and all his brothers ribbed him for it. He'd had such a great childhood growing up with all of them, and he'd never wanted more than his life in Coral Canyon.

He couldn't even comprehend a life like the one Lily had lived, the places she'd seen, or the things she'd done. It wasn't jealousy that streamed through him, but definitely anxiety. He wasn't sure he would ever be enough for her, not when she'd probably experienced much grander things that this lodge, this quaint piece of land with a handful of horses in the stables.

He smiled back at Andrew and said, "I'm just going to take a break."

"You're doing the Christmas tree this year, right?" Graham asked as Beau passed him. "Here at the lodge?"

"Yeah, I'm still planning on it." And he had quite the tradition to live up to. Since Graham had come home and hosted the first Christmas at this lodge, there had been a huge tree, with a lighting ceremony and a family dinner on Christmas Eve. They exchanged gifts, and each brother had hosted it over the past three years.

Beau supposed that he would be in charge of this particular Whittaker tradition for the foreseeable future if he wanted it to continue. After all, he had no plans to vacate the lodge. He didn't have a girlfriend with a ranch of her own. Or a new wife in California. Or someone in town to move in with once he got married.

Another keen sense of foolishness hit him as he realized that the woman he was currently falling for probably wouldn't stay a moment past the time he settled her last case.

He hated these poisonous thoughts, but he didn't know how to cleanse them from his mind. Maybe if he spoke with Lily, she'd help him see reason and he could make sense of what to do next.

So he put on his boots, his coat, his gloves, his hat, and he followed the sidewalk down to the stables. She stood at Dandelion's stall, whispering to her about something. Maybe the song she was going to write once she returned to Nashville, to her real life.

"Hey," he said, surprised his voice didn't betray the negative feelings bouncing around inside him.

She twisted toward him and graced him with a small smile. "Just couldn't stay away, could you?"

He shrugged one shoulder. "How are you feeling about Kent?"

Nervous energy radiated off of her, and Second to Caroline, the horse closest to him shuffled its hooves. "I think I may have done something stupid," she said.

Beau took a step closer to her. "What's that?"

"I called my grandparents," she said, wringing her hands around and around one another. "They didn't say my name, but Pops called me 'Princess,' and if Kent has been listening at all, he'll know...."

Beau felt like he'd swallowed too much salt water. His stomach writhed as he took a few steps toward her. She advanced toward him too, and when they met a moment later, Beau simply took her hands in his.

"I guess we'll deal with what we have to," he said. "But there's not much we can do about it today, is there?"

"Has your friend called you again?"

"No, but he said he would when he knew anything." Beau stroked her hair off her face. "And I'll keep working on these last two cases." He wanted to promise her that they'd win, that this would all be over soon, but he didn't know if that was true or not, so he said nothing of the sort.

They swayed together and he asked, "Did you want to help me with the Christmas tree this year? My family sort of has this lighting tradition, and we need to get a tree up and decorated in the foyer."

"Sure," she said. "But I need to finish the stained glass first."

"How long do you have on that?" he asked.

"I think I can get it done this week." She laid her cheek right against his chest, and all those doubts about their relationship dried right up. Beau wasn't sure why he couldn't believe Lily liked him. All of her actions seemed to indicate that she did. But so had Deirdre's.

"Still no contact with your sisters?" Beau asked.

"No."

"Anything else I should know?"

"I don't think so. I just couldn't help myself," she said, pushing back and looking at him. "It's Thanksgiving, and they don't have anyone else." She looked so earnest and sincere, and Beau's heart squeezed a little bit more.

"It's okay that you called," he said. "I'll make sure I get in touch with Paul Glamp in the morning and let him know. He'll go by and talk to your grandparents, sweep their house for bugs, and then we'll know." He rubbed her back. "Okay?"

She nodded. "Okay."

"Great, now unless you're dyin' to go for a ride, I think we should get back to the house. There's this riveting game of Hearts going on in the dining room."

Lily giggled, and Beau bent down to kiss her, taking the opportunity to do so before returning to the house full of people and the complete lack of privacy.

BEAU SHIFTED another piece of paper, trying to find some detail he'd overlooked. Kent had filed to have lifetime access to a portion of the royalties of the Everett Sisters albums that had been made during the time of his marriage to Lily, claiming that he'd put up with the long hours that Lily worked and all the travel and that the sacrifices he'd made for those albums should be rewarded.

This was a new filing to a case that had awarded him a lump sum five years ago for those albums.

"He can't take a percentage off the top forever," Beau said to himself. "But how do I get a judge to dismiss this completely?" He'd been planning to use some of the same arguments he had for the alimony case, but he wondered now if he needed more than that. Something a bit stronger.

So he went back to his notebook, scratching out notes and questions he needed to find out about Kent. About mid-morning, he called Sheriff Glamp and asked some questions and got Paul to send a couple of officers over to the Pettit's house just to make sure everything was okay.

He heard Lily hammering away at something in the living room, and he got up and stretched his back. She wanted him to warn her when he came in while she was working, so he called, "Can I come in?" as he walked down the hall.

"Give me a minute," she called back.

"Coffee?" he asked, taking a small peek into the living room. He couldn't really see more than Lily standing on a ladder and holding a piece of green glass.

"I brought you coffee an hour ago," she said, and Beau turned into the kitchen, wondering if that was really true. He hadn't had a sip of coffee yet, nor had he seen Lily yet that morning.

Had he? He'd been so involved in the files and ideas that he hadn't noticed much of anything.

The kitchen was empty, and the coffee in the pot was old. He washed it out and set a new pot to brew. He pulled open the fridge and pulled out leftover turkey and mashed potatoes. Returning for the gravy, he put together a breakfast of champions for the day after Thanksgiving, glad Celia hadn't sent all the leftovers home with his brothers.

With a plate of food and a fresh cup of coffee, Beau settled at the bar and started eating. Five minutes later, Lily entered the kitchen, wiping her hands on a paper towel. "Morning," he said and took another bite of potatoes.

"Good morning, times two," she said. She collapsed onto the barstool next to him and leaned against his bicep. "You seemed pretty involved in your computer this morning."

"Yeah," he said, not wanting to admit he hadn't even noticed her when she'd come in. "How's the window coming along?"

"Great." She smiled at him and got up and poured herself a cup of coffee.

"I think I'm going to go into town this morning," he said.

"It's almost lunchtime," she said. "And it's pouring rain. Snow in the forecast."

"It would be a quick trip," he said.

"Promise you won't peek at the window when you drive up," she said. "It's almost done, and I don't want you to see it."

"I won't," he said.

She walked by him and swept a kiss along his temple and said, "Okay, I'm going to go shower then."

He watched her leave and then he finished his breakfast-slash-lunch. The drive down the canyon was filled with driving rain, which lessened the further into town he went. He stopped by his mother's place first, a bit dismayed to see a car that wasn't hers in the driveway.

He stayed in his SUV and watched the windows, thinking he should call first so he didn't interrupt something that would embarrass either one of them. His phone chimed before he could get the call sent, and it was his mother.

I see you out there. You gonna come in?

Is Jason here? he sent back. *I don't want to interrupt anything. It's the grocery delivery.*

The door opened, and a young man came bustling out, his hood up over his head. He ran down the sidewalk and practically leapt into his car. Beau copied him in reverse, bursting into the warmth of his mother's house.

"Wow, it's raining harder than it looks," he said, shaking the water from his cowboy hat.

His mother stood in the kitchen, unloading her groceries. "What brings you down to town?"

Beau walked into the kitchen and sat at the bar. "Just wanted to see you, Mom."

She gave him a narrow-eyed glance and pulled out a can of beans. "That's not good."

"What? I can't come visit my mother?" He grinned at her and reached for the bag of tortilla chips she hadn't put away yet.

"How are things with Lily?"

"The cases are going okay," he said, not wanting to get into all the details of what he hadn't been able to figure out yet.

"I meant your relationship with her."

"I—we're not—"

She rolled her eyes and said, "Oh, come on. Everyone knows you two are dating."

"How?" Beau ripped open the chips and took out a handful.

"Well, for one, you invited Andrew and Becca up for movie night."

"So?"

"So that wasn't a date?"

"I don't think anyone ever used the word date," Beau said immediately stuffing his mouth full of chips.

"But you are dating her." She turned and put her canned goods in the pantry. "Right?"

When she looked him in the eye, Beau couldn't lie to her. "Yes, all right? Yes, we're dating. Sort of."

His mom shook her head, a loving smile on her face. "Oh, Beau."

"I'm an idiot, aren't I?" He pushed the chips away.

"No," she said but she didn't add to it.

"Her ex is in Jackson," Beau said. "I'm trying to keep her safe and win her cases."

"And she's doing a stained glass window for your house, and you're falling for her."

"I'm not, Mom." Beau stood up. "Honestly, I'm not." But he wasn't sure if he was or not. He could be, but it was happening quite a bit slower than his fall with Deirdre. "She's a big celebrity, and there's no way she's staying somewhere like Coral Canyon."

He wished the truthfulness of his words didn't echo quite so loudly in his ears or fill the rafters of the house.

"I have to go," he said, heading for the front door. "I have some files at the courthouse I need to look at."

EIGHTEEN

LILY WENT RIGHT BACK to work on the stained glass window after she showered, though the smell of the solder was giving her a headache. She wanted to get this window done for some reason. Maybe it was because Beau had mentioned a big Christmas tree project, and she wanted to be available for that.

Or maybe she knew her time at the lodge was coming to an end and she didn't want to leave her window unfinished.

She cut the blue cathedral glass to fit the triangle she needed for the middle of the E on the name *Whittaker*. She loved the logo she'd contracted through another email address with an artist. The last name was made of beautiful glass in an array of colors, and she'd finished those first.

The horseshoe had come together nicely, as had the rainbow. She just had the finishing touches to complete, and then she needed to go through the cleaning process to make sure when she revealed the design, the sun could truly illuminate each piece.

She liked the silence in the house, and she could tell Celia, Bree, and everyone else had gone home last night. When they were in the lodge, it had a different presence. Lily liked them both, but something was still unsettled inside her.

Beau hadn't said anything about her grandparents, which Lily had assumed was a good thing. So she hadn't asked. Rose and Violet had both emailed last night, and Lily thought through their messages as she fitted the glass into place and melted a piece of solder in exactly the right place.

She'd forgotten how much she enjoyed creating, as she hadn't written a song or anything creative in a long time. Sure, she had lots of lines typed into her phone, but nothing had come together into a song in a while.

When she caught sight of Beau's SUV coming through the parking lot, she hung the paper over the section she was working on and climbed down the ladder.

The garage door slammed the moment her foot hit the floor, and she wiped her hands down her thighs.

She watched him hang his keys on the hook and take off his hat. She'd forgotten how long his hair was on top, as she normally only saw the shaved sides outside of his cowboy hat.

"You got a haircut," she said.

He turned and faced her, and he looked tired. "I sure did." He took a few slow steps toward her. "And I spent a lot of time at the courthouse."

A twinge of guilt hit her, but then she reminded herself

that she was paying him to win her cases. "Learn anything good?"

"I got a couple of things," he said generally, and Lily didn't press for more. She'd learned that he kept his legal strategies mostly to himself and just told her what she needed to know, when she needed to know it.

He lifted a bag. "I brought lunch."

"As if we don't have enough food in the fridge." She grinned at him. "The lodge is different with just the two of us here, don't you think?"

"Is it?" He veered into the kitchen and set the white paper bag on the counter. "Different good, or different bad?"

She stepped beside him and watched him pull out white Styrofoam containers that smelled very much like her favorite Chinese food. Her mouth watered, and her stomach reminded her that she had only drunk coffee for breakfast.

"Just...different." She slipped her hand through his elbow, her heart thumping weirdly once and then settling down. She really liked Beau, and she wanted to talk to him about something.

"My sisters emailed last night."

"Oh?" He flipped open the first container to reveal the Red China spicy chicken she loved, as well as ham fried rice.

She picked up one of the plastic forks and tugged the container toward her while he opened a second one, this time with an egg roll inside.

"This one's yours," he said, but he plucked the egg roll from his container and put it in her lid.

"Thank you," she said. "Rose said Vi's solo album isn't going well, and the producers are asking when I'll be back."

Beau nodded. "Sorry about your sister's album."

"I'm sure it's fine." She didn't need to explain all the different distinctions that were used to measure an album's success. No, Vi hadn't gone platinum, or even gold, but selling a hundred thousand records was nothing to sneeze at.

"What are you going to do?" he asked.

She looked at him, but he wouldn't meet her gaze. She really wanted to look into his eyes, as if the answers to what she should do would be written there, in his dark depths.

When he never would focus on anything but his chicken, she looked away too. "I like writing songs," she said. "I'm a creative person."

Several seconds of silence went by. "I sense a but," he said.

There was definitely a but. Problem was, Lily wasn't sure she should say what came behind it. She felt like she was at a crossroads in her life and it was time to choose.

"But I really like it here," she said, employing her bravery. "I like the horses. I like this lodge. I like you."

That got him to look at her, and Lily shrugged, the honesty already flowing between them. "But—"

"I don't want to hear what comes after this one," Beau said, a sad and playful smile on his face.

"Ha ha." Lily nudged him with her shoulder. "I just think maybe this isn't where I'm supposed to be."

"Why would you think that?"

"I don't know. I've always lived near my sisters. We write songs, record them, and tour together. This totally different than that."

"I get that."

He said he did, but Lily wasn't sure he *could* get it.

"And I don't want to put you in danger."

"Lily," he said, and something warm flowed through her blood at the tender, husky way he said her name. "I am not in danger because of you."

"What if Kent comes here, and to get to me, he goes through Celia? Or your mother?" Lily didn't have to look at his face to feel him flinch.

"I'm sure that won't happen."

"You've never met Kent."

"Is he violent? You've never said that."

"No, he's proper," Lily said. "But he's not afraid to hire people who are below board."

"But he has no money."

Lily let the argument drop then, mostly because Beau was right. Maybe she was worrying about nothing.

"I didn't answer either of my sisters," she said. "I'm thinking of telling them about us."

Beau met her eye again. "Is that right? What are you going to tell them?"

She grinned at him. "That I'm dating this really great guy, and we're going to decorate a Christmas tree together."

He groaned and said, "Don't remind me."

"That you're great? Fine, I'll never mention it again."

He laughed, slung his arm around her, and said, "I think you're pretty great too."

She smiled and received his kiss willingly, glad she'd confessed some things to him and praying that when it came time to really make a decision, she could make the right one.

❅

"ALL RIGHT, ARE YOU READY?" Lily perched on the ladder, her hand already positioned on the brown butcher paper she'd been using to keep the stained glass concealed. Bree, Celia, and Beau stood together near the doorway, as Lily had instructed them. That way they'd have the best view of the design.

Her stomach rioted against the idea of pulling down the tape, and she adjusted her fingers on the paper. She told herself over and over again that Beau would love it.

"We're ready," Beau said, an encouraging smile on his face. Lily took another moment to memorize him like that, his eyes bright and hopeful, that cowboy hat tipped back so he could see her near the ceiling.

"Okay." She pushed out her breath and tugged on the paper, the tape nearest her coming loose instantly. She had to pull a little harder to get the piece way down on the other end to pop free, but when it did, the brown paper drifted down to reveal the window.

She'd used cathedral glass and standard gray solder to form the design over the existing window. It had a long, curved arch along the top, and she'd done most of the glass up there in shades of blue and green, which were calming.

Light splashed onto the floor below, but Lily couldn't look away from Beau's face. Wonder crossed it, and maybe something like pure awe. She wasn't sure if he liked it or not.

The word WHITTAKER ran across the straight bottom of the window, with the rainbow over the curve of the R at the end, and the horseshoe hung on one of the points of the W at the beginning.

The letters were done in a shade of black that still let in plenty of light, and while Lily could see all the flaws in the window, Beau said, "Wow. It's stunning."

He came forward and extended his hand for her to hold as she made her way down the ladder, and he took her effortlessly into his arms once she'd reached the floor. He kissed her quickly, apparently not caring that they had onlookers, and said, "I love it."

"Yeah?" Lily turned in his arms and faced the window, trying to see it from his perspective. Down here, the flaws weren't quite so obvious, and she supposed it did look nice.

"It's wonderful," Celia said with a sniffle. Before Lily could turn to look at her, the older woman left the room.

"It'll be even better in the summer," Lily said. "When the sun is hotter and brighter."

"I love it," Bree said with a smile. She touched Lily's arm, and when Lily looked at her, she found kindness in her eyes. "The guests will like it too."

"I went with the last name," Lily explained. "Because I figured you Whittaker brothers would keep the lodge. Maybe rename it, but always keep it."

"I plan to keep it," Beau said. "I should probably talk to Graham about that. He bought it, years ago after our dad died."

Lily tightened her arm around him, and said, "Let's go see what Celia whipped up for this celebration." She hadn't specifically asked Celia to bake anything, but when they entered the kitchen, she had strawberry shortcake on the counter as she piped perfect star-shaped dollops of whipped cream onto it.

Lily ate the delicious dessert and basked in all the compliments from the others. While the wind howled through the Wyoming landscape, she felt warm and secure inside Whiskey Mountain Lodge. With Beau. With this new family she was making.

A few days later, she and Beau wandered through the Christmas trees in the parking lot at the hardware store. Lily wore her hair up under one of Beau's ballcaps, an oversized jacket, and a pair of sunglasses. No one questioned her on the last accessory, because it had been snowing for days and the sun had finally broken through, causing a blinding glint to reflect off of everything.

"I like this one," she said, pointing to a tree hardly bigger than herself.

"It's too small, sweetheart." Beau chuckled and pointed toward the far side of the lot. "That foyer is huge. We need at least twenty feet."

"How are we supposed to decorate a tree twenty feet tall?"

"One ornament at a time." He took her hand and led her through the much smaller trees to the giants on the side. There were only six to choose from, as apparently the twenty-footers weren't that popular.

They all looked the same to her, and she let Beau pick the one he thought was "the most robust." He paid for the tree, and she watched while he and two other men hefted it on top of his SUV.

Back at the lodge, she had to help him, Bree, and

Graham get the tree in the house, but then she stood back and watched as some of the red, blue, and yellow light from the stained glass window danced across the pine needles.

"Looks great," she said, noting that the top of the tree barely reached the top of the stairs. They probably could've gotten a thirty foot tree and still been fine.

"Do you want to start decorating today?" he asked.

"Not really," she said. "We have plenty of time, right?" She admired the bare tree just the way it was, wondering why it needed to be dressed up at all.

"Sure, yeah," he said. "I think we need new lights anyway. I can get some this weekend, and then we'll get 'er done."

Lily stayed in the living room while he went down the hall to his office. Celia wasn't at the lodge today, and Bree stopped by to say she was running down to town to get a few things for the guests that would be there the following evening.

She had just made herself a cup of hot chocolate and settled next to the tree when someone knocked on the big front door a few feet from her. It sounded like a child's knock, barely loud enough to hear.

Glancing toward the hallway, she expected to find Beau standing there. Or at least coming. Nervous energy fired through her like fireworks. Was he expecting someone? Should she answer the door?

She waited, thinking maybe she'd imagined the sound. But it came again—soft yet insistent.

She couldn't fathom leaving a child outside with the wind driving the snow to and fro the way it was. She sent a quick text to Beau—*are you expecting someone at the lodge?*—before she got up to open the front door.

"Hello—" Her voice turned to glass and shattered when she saw a tall, gangly man with chestnut brown hair on the porch. He was not a child. He could surely knock harder than he had been.

Behind her, she heard Daisy bark, and a flutter of hope entered her chest.

The man turned toward her, and Kent's mouth turned upward as if he was genuinely excited to see her. "Hello, Lily."

Her mug of hot chocolate fell toward the tile floor, smashing into shards, hot liquid, and spongy marshmallows. She felt frozen, but she managed to start to swing the door closed. If she could just get it locked, she'd have a few seconds to get Beau and figure something out.

But Kent put his foot in the way, and the door wouldn't budge.

NINETEEN

BEAU RECEIVED several messages at the same time, and it took him a moment to tear his attention from the email he'd just gotten.

Sheriff Glamp had confirmed several days ago that Kent was in Jackson Hole for the foreseeable future, not just for the holidays. And the county recorder had just emailed him to let him know that a man fitting Kent's description had just inquired about where Beau's offices were.

So Kent knew he was Lily's lawyer. He was tenacious and resourceful too, if the text from Karla at the diner was any indication. *A man just asked around all my tables for where you lived. He knows.*

Beau's heart pounded in his chest. Kent felt moments away, and he pushed his chair back to stand up. He tapped on Lily's text, and his blood went cold.

No, he was not expecting anyone. He bolted toward the

door as Daisy started barking. Not good. Definitely not good.

"Don't open it," he called, jogging down the hall. Everything in his world felt off-kilter, especially when he skidded to a stop in the living room and took in the scene before him.

Lily had already answered the door, Daisy at her side.

Kent was already inside the lodge.

Beau had failed.

He continued forward anyway, stepping between Kent and Lily though there was no room for him there. He forced her back toward the tree, and thankfully, she went, taking the Rotwieller with her. "You can't come in," he said. "This is private property."

Kent simply stared at him, a placid smile on his face.

"Please back up," Beau said again, his voice with a bit more bite.

"She invited me in," Kent said.

"No, I didn't," Lily said, and Beau was glad she had enough fight left in her to speak.

"You're not welcome here, and you can't come in," Beau said. "If you don't leave right now, I'll call the police."

"She's my wife."

"*Ex*-wife," Lily said.

"She has a restraining order against you," Beau said.

That got Kent to look at him. "Excuse me?"

"Filed yesterday morning. If you don't leave in the next ten seconds, I'm afraid you'll be spending the night in jail."

An anger so violent entered Kent's face that Beau braced himself to get punched. But he would take the hit if he had to. In that moment, nose-to-nose with Kent Gulbrandsen, Beau knew he'd fallen in love with Lily.

"I didn't get notified of a restraining order," he said through clenched teeth.

"That's because you weren't at the hotel in Jackson Hole," Beau said calmly. "Go ahead and call down to the police department here. Or over to Sheriff Glamp's office. You'll see I'm telling the truth."

Kent pulled out his phone as if he'd stand in Beau's warm foyer and make his calls.

"Out there," Beau said, nodding toward the door. "All the way to the road, in fact. This is private property to that road, and you can't be within one hundred yards of Miss Lily Everett."

Kent snarled, but he spun and marched out of the front door. Beau wasted no time in bringing it closed and locking it. He turned back to Lily, his adrenaline still pumping through him with the speed of a freight train.

"I'm sorry," she said, tears springing to her eyes. "He knocked so softly, and I thought maybe it was Bailey or another child."

Beau gathered Lily into his arms and shushed her. "It's fine."

"I didn't know you filed a restraining order."

"Kent's been getting closer and closer," he said. "I got some emails and messages this morning—literally moments ago—so I'm glad I did." He'd made the decision on the spot, while at the courthouse the previous day. A restraining order would indicate Lily didn't feel safe, and that could very well help them with the last remaining case Beau was still working on.

And now it had gotten Kent out of the lodge too. He moved to the door and found Kent crossing the parking lot with long strides. "I don't think he'll come back."

"But he knows where I am," Lily said. "I have to go."

Beau turned back to her, glad he had a hold of her hand or he feared she'd already be gone. "No, you don't have to go. That's the point of the restraining order. It keeps him away. You're safe here."

She shook her head, her fingers slipping out of his. He felt like he was teetering on the edge of a very high cliff, and if she left Whiskey Mountain Lodge, he'd be falling forever. "Don't go," he said, his voice strained and full of emotion.

I love you. Please don't go.

He could've said the words, but he didn't.

I only have one more case to finish, and I'm so close. Please stay.

Lily's tears slid down her cheeks. "I can't put you in danger."

"I'm not in danger." Now he sounded like an angry dog, barking the sentence at her. His phone buzzed and chimed, but he didn't look at it. He couldn't seem to look away from Lily.

"It's time to go back to Nashville anyway," she said.

"No," Beau said, a definite note of pleading in the two-letter word.

"You'll finish the case, and then it will all be over anyway." Lily threw up her hands as if she had no idea what to do, frustration etching itself into every line of her face. "We both know I can't stay here forever."

"Why can't you?" He took a step forward and reached for her, ready to say all the words that needed to be said.

She backed up too, looking at him helplessly. "That was never the plan."

"Make a new plan."

"I can't, Beau." She took another step backward, and then another one. When she reached the doorway, she turned and walked down the hall, her footsteps sounding very final though she didn't even wear shoes.

Beau stood in the living room, the slight scent of the pine tree beside him making his stomach sour. Or maybe that was the china all over the floor, or the spilled hot chocolate inching nearer to his boots.

Or maybe his heart was breaking again, and he simply couldn't stop it.

BEAU WANTED to hide in the office or his bedroom while Lily left Whiskey Mountain Lodge, but he wasn't a ten-year-old, and he thought maybe he'd find the bravery he needed to speak.

So he followed Lily outside, glad when there were no other cars parked in the lot. Kent hadn't come back in, obviously confirming the restraining order Beau had put in place. Something seethed just beneath his skin. There was no guarantee that he wasn't sitting in his rental, just down the hill where he couldn't be seen from here.

But that warning from Beau's mouth had fallen on deaf ears. Lily was determined to leave, and though she continued to sniffle and weep, her resolve on the matter seemed absolute.

He hefted her two bags into the truck beside the one she'd already put there and slammed it closed. "Anything else?"

She readjusted her purse on her arm and shook her head.

"You don't have to do this," he said. "We haven't even decorated the tree."

Fresh tears started, and she reached up and cradled his face. "I know. I'm so sorry."

But was she really?

"Talk to me," he said. "I don't understand."

"This...we...." She shook her head, her pretty blue eyes torturing him with the sadness they held. "I have another life, and it's time I get back to it."

The breath got sucked out of his body as if her words were a vacuum and she'd plugged the hose right into his lungs. Deirdre had wanted her old life back too. Beau obviously wasn't a strong enough influence for anyone to stay and make a new life with him.

Fury roared within him, and he started nodding in short bursts. "Fine."

"Beau."

"Don't," he bit out. "I get it. This isn't your life. You've never wanted this life. We've always been temporary."

If only his stupid heart would get those memos and listen to them.

"Go on, then," he said. "Good luck in Nashville." He turned and walked away, calling over his shoulder. "I'll need to contact you about the last case, so after you ditch your phone and get a new one, do be kind enough to text me at least once."

He couldn't help the pettiness in his voice, though he didn't like it and wished he could act differently. But he couldn't get to the house fast enough either. He ran the last few steps to the stairs and took them two at a time.

Once inside, on the still sticky floor, he slammed the heavy wooden door and locked it before he leaned his back against it.

He sucked at the air, the panic and desperation coiling together to make a tornado of negativity in his core.

"I can't...live...like this," he gasped, trying trying trying to understand what was so bad about him that he couldn't get a woman to stay in Coral Canyon. Why couldn't he meet someone like Lily at the grocery store? Someone who already lived in town and wanted to be here?

One tiny ray of hope shone through the dark clouds descending on him, and that was that he hadn't confessed the full depth of his feelings for Lily. She didn't get to know he loved her, and that she'd broken his heart. He'd given Deirdre that satisfaction, but he would not give it to Lily.

He slid down the door and sat on the floor, the lodge bigger and emptier than it had ever been. The Christmas tree in front of him seemed stupid without any lights, tinsel, or ornaments on it, but Beau wasn't feeling much Christmas spirit at the moment.

A day passed. Then two. Beau fed the horses, and made coffee for himself in the mornings. He texted Celia and said he didn't need her help until Christmastime. He didn't want to explain about Lily, or the fact that he hadn't even gotten out the boxes of Christmas décor.

Bree showed up when there were guests, and she eyed him as he sat in front of his laptop in the office until he snapped, "What?"

"Nothing." She got up and left, and when she didn't come back, Beau's guilt took over. He texted her an apology, and she responded with *I understand. Is Lily coming back?*

Beau didn't want to admit that she wasn't, so he ignored Bree's message and focused on the case. The restraining order would certainly help. As would the new statements Beau had procured from a pet store in Hollywood, where Kent had apparently applied for a job. He'd gotten it, but never shown up for work.

So he obviously wasn't following the judge's ruling from the alimony cases, and Beau added those statements to his case file.

He got out his best suit and took it to the cleaners. He wanted it to be ready if he had to appear in court, as a settlement started to become farther and farther from reality.

He did not decorate the tree. Or try to get in touch with Lily.

Sheriff Glamp had said Kent had cleared out of town, and no one in Coral Canyon had seen him either. So he was either smarter than Beau had given him credit for and had taken the restraining order seriously, or he knew Lily wasn't here and had followed her back to Nashville.

The restraining order would work there too, but not if Lily didn't enforce it.

One morning, only a week before Christmas, Beau's

exhaustion kept him in bed past his usual rising time. He laid there, his head turned toward the window, and watched the snow drift down. Coral Canyon was under almost three feet now, but Beau found he didn't care.

He didn't care about much of anything anymore.

A loud banging noise had him jolting to a sitting position, as did the clomping of booted feet as they came toward his bedroom door.

"Beau!" Graham called, but knowing that it was his brother and not a thief did not comfort Beau. He didn't want to talk to anyone. His texts saying as much should've clued everyone in, as should've his complete absence from church or a social life at all these past few weeks.

More banging on the door, and then it opened. Graham stood there, dripping water from the brim of his cowboy hat onto Beau's perfectly clean floors.

"What are you doing?" his brother asked.

"Sleeping." Beau laid back down. "Leave me alone, Graham."

"I'll take care of the horses," he said, and he did as Beau asked and left.

Beau wanted him to come back almost the moment the back door slammed closed, and he pressed his eyes shut so he could try to make sense of things.

He couldn't.

When he was up, he wanted to be down. But when he got down, he wanted to be up again. He didn't want Graham there, but as soon as he left, he wanted his brother to come back.

Frustration filled him from top to bottom, and he prayed,

not for the first time, that he could somehow find his way through this maze he'd gotten trapped in.

The Lord usually provided a light for Beau, some way for him to see the end goal and work toward it. But he felt like he'd been abandoned, and there simply wasn't going to be any help this time.

Graham did return a while later, this time with a cup of coffee. "Laney said she'd come decorate the tree." He set the mug on Beau's bedside table and took up residence in the armchair.

"Don't you have to work?" he asked.

Graham just chuckled and said, "Why didn't you tell me Lily had left?"

"No point," Beau muttered, hoping this would be a very short conversation.

"Is she coming back?"

"Not unless she has to appear in court."

"Where is she?"

"Nashville."

Graham made a noise of disapproval, and that almost sent Beau over the edge. Sure, *he* could be mad at Lily, but he didn't want anyone else to think badly of her.

"Well, why are you still here?" Graham asked next.

Beau lifted his head and looked at his brother. "What do you mean?"

"I mean, it's obvious you're in love with her. Why don't you go find her and make sure she knows?"

It sounded so simple. "It's not that simple," Beau said.

"Isn't it?"

"No." He sighed and swung his legs over the side of the bed. "I'm fine. I'm getting up."

"About the tree lighting—"

"I'll get it done," Beau said, flashing his brother a dark look. "Okay? Leave me alone. I still have six days before Christmas Eve." And he had no idea how he was going to survive them. Probably how he'd been suffering through the minutes and hours of the past two weeks.

Or had it been three? Four?

Beau had no idea, and another wave of helplessness engulfed him, almost driving him back to bed. He stood instead, stretched his back, and said, "Now, if you could just point me in the direction of where the Christmas ornaments are stored...."

TWENTY

LILY CHECKED out of the hotel where she'd been for less than twelve hours by leaving her room key on the dresser in the room. Over the course of the last week, she hadn't stayed in the same place for more than one night. She'd kept her hair hidden, unable to bring herself to dye it. Her long, almost white hair was one of the trademarks of the Everett Sisters, and she couldn't cut or color it. She actually had a contract not to.

So she smoothed it back and tied a scarf over her head, covering that with the hood from her sweatshirt. When she was satisfied that not a wisp of her hair was showing, she stepped out of the room and forced herself to walk calmly to the rental car.

She'd left hers at the bus station in Jackson Hole, hidden in the bathroom to call her manager about using the business credit card to rent something inconspicuous to drive back to Nashville.

"Does this mean you're coming back?" Shawn had asked, and Lily had confirmed it. She'd said she'd be in Nashville for the New Year, and she still had a couple of weeks to get there.

The thought of spending Christmas by herself made her chest cinch. She wanted to turn the car around and head back to Wyoming right now. She could and if she drove straight through, she could be back by nightfall. Instead, she turned the car toward Kansas City and drove as if she were going into the city to work. She'd spend lunch at some run down diner or bistro, and then she'd hunt for a hotel in a smaller town a few hundred miles closer to Nashville.

She didn't want to go straight there, though if she just got in the car and put the pedal to the metal, she could see her sisters by morning.

She was sort of hoping the highway would give her the answers she sought. Problem was, she wasn't even sure she knew the questions to ask, so getting the answers was nigh to impossible.

"Help me," she said aloud, glad she could still speak, that her voice worked. She hadn't been using her vocal chords in quite the way she used to, and she began to hum and then sing one of the Everett Sister's most popular ballads.

When she finished that one, she went down the set list for their third album, the one that had broken the record for the most amount of tour money earned by a musical group. They'd broken their own record on the next tour, but their fifth album hadn't been as popular.

Lily sang through a few more songs, each one calming her until she felt like she could go ten more miles. Then ten more. Before she knew it, she was only an hour outside of St. Louis. She decided to stop there, choosing a big city over a small one for tonight.

And she'd be in Nashville by tomorrow, if Rose didn't email her about Kent. Lily didn't know where he'd gone, and she hadn't seen him.

She'd had three phones since leaving Coral Canyon, and she'd emailed Beau with yet another email address that he hadn't yet responded to. So she still had one case pending, and she almost hoped it would drag on and on, because then she'd have a tie to him. A connection.

If he finished her legal work, she'd never have a legitimate reason to contact him.

"Sure you would," she told herself. "You like him." Lily stopped speaking, because she really disliked lying to herself out loud. She more than liked Beau Whittaker, and way down deep she knew it. She didn't want to let that truth up too far, or she might call him and tell him with real words.

"He'll never forgive you." She sighed and leaned her head against the window. She decided she couldn't drive anymore and got off the freeway when she saw the first hotel sign. She checked in, using cash she'd gotten in Denver, and made it to her assigned room without incident.

She hadn't meant to use the exact same reason as his previous girlfriend and client had used to break up with him. But it had worked, no matter how much hurt she'd seen in his eyes. No matter if she hadn't wanted to say it or not.

No matter that it wasn't really true.

"Oh, it's at least partially true," she said to the empty room. Yes, she had loved the lodge, and the little of

Coral Canyon that she'd seen. She had wanted to stay and decorate that gigantic Christmas tree, and experience the tree lighting ceremony with Beau and his family.

She wondered if he'd gone in her bedroom yet, or if he'd let Bree take care of the linens. She'd already gotten him a Christmas gift, smuggled into the lodge by Celia after one of her trips to town, and she'd left the present on the nightstand in her bedroom.

She hoped he hadn't gotten it yet, not that he had and had then decided not to email her a thank you.

"Doesn't matter," she whispered as she dragged her suitcase closer to the bed. She unzipped it and got out what she needed to take a shower, hoping the hot water could help her relax but fearing that she wouldn't be able to do that until her cases were settled and she'd figured out what to say to Beau.

SHE PULLED up to the gate where Vi lived, a tremor of anticipation skipping through her system. After rolling down the window, she pressed the button and waited. Vi had a doorman that checked all traffic in and out of the house, and his voice came through the speaker with a distinct English accent.

"Who may I say is here?" Rupert always asked the same thing. He was never impolite, even when he had to turn someone away.

"It's Lily, Rupert," she said, pulling her shades down

slightly so he could see her eyes. "I'm not sure if Vi knew I'd be here today or not."

"One moment."

Lily sighed and leaned her head against the back of her seat. She felt spent, like she didn't have anything inside of her to give. But when Rupert said, "Please pull forward," in the same voice she'd heard him use countless times before, she found the strength to do just that.

Move forward.

As she eased her rental car down the meticulously land-scaped lane and around the bend to the front door, she hoped her reunion would be joyous. Her sisters spilled from the double-wide doors as she put the car in park, and she could see their jubilation plainly on their faces.

It was enough to spur her from the car, a shriek riding the back of her throat.

"Lily!" Rose laughed as she flew down the stairs ahead of Vi and slammed into Lily, grabbing onto her and giggling like a little girl.

"You're home." Vi engulfed them all in a hug, and Lily put one arm around each of them, her tears instant and hot in her eyes and on her face. Oh, how she'd missed them. There was nowhere as comforting as her sister's arms, and she held them tight, tight, tight.

When she pulled away, she wasn't the only one crying, thank goodness.

"You've ruined my perfect makeup day," Vi said, wiping her eyes. "My eyeliner was so crisp." She gave a tear-filled laugh, and Lily just beamed at her.

"You look great," she told her sister. Vi did not have a

contract for her hair color, but she kept it the color of ripe wheat. Lily knew that came out of a bottle, but Vi had never told anyone that but her family. "I love you guys."

Rose slipped her arm around Lily and hugged her close. "It's so good to see you. Come tell us everything." And when Rose said that, Lily knew she'd have to do exactly that. Another wave of exhaustion rolled over her, but the moment she stepped inside her sister's house, she felt the same peace that had existed in the lodge in Coral Canyon.

"So is everything settled?" Vi asked, curling her slender legs under her body.

"Almost." Lily pushed out her breath as she sat, her eyes drifting closed too. "One case left."

"And you came home?" The surprise in Vi's voice wasn't hard to find.

Lily opened her eyes to catch the tail end of an exchanged look between Rose and Vi. They were going to find out everything anyway, because Lily didn't keep a whole lot of secrets from her sisters. It made recording and working together difficult.

"I hired the best lawyer in Wyoming," she said.

"Of course you did," Rose said, an obvious encouragement for Lily to keep talking.

"And he also happened to be this rugged, sexy mountain man with a law degree."

"Oh, boy," Vi said. "How is it that she gets to meet all the interesting men when she's supposed to be in hiding?" She looked at Rose as if she'd just asked a serious question, then tossed a playful smile at Lily.

But Lily couldn't smile back. Her heart hurt too much. "I

left him there. Kent showed up, and I freaked out, and I left the cowboy lawyer in Wyoming."

Several beats of silence passed, broken when Rose said, "Get her her guitar, Vi. Let's see what she's been working on."

Lily didn't want to tell them she hadn't been working on anything. The Lily she'd been when she'd left them here in Nashville was a workaholic. Someone always jotting down lyrics or finding new ways to rhyme.

Vi got up and left the room, and Lily looked at Rose. "I haven't played a guitar in over a year."

Rose just blinked at her. Asked, "What?"

"I didn't work on any songs while I was gone."

Vi returned, Lily's guitar in her hand. The veneer on the front gleamed as if they'd had it polished weekly while she'd been gone. Guilt gutted her, and she accepted the instrument from her sister.

"She says she hasn't played," Rose said. "You haven't written one song?"

Lily shook her head, taking a few moments to get the guitar settled in her lap the way she liked it. Playing the guitar felt natural to her, and her fingers found their places on the board easily. She plucked, knowing she'd have some serious pain until her calluses reformed.

"I wrote down some lyrics at first," Lily said above the low guitar music. "But nothing serious."

Until Beau. Then she'd had all kinds of lyrics come to her. She hadn't organized them into anything resembling a song though.

"Well, it's time to get serious," Vi said. "Lee said he can't wait to see you in the studio in January."

Lily glanced at Vi, an internal groan forming in her chest. Instead of letting it out, she said, "I think I might have a song for Beau."

"Beau?" Rose asked. "Is he your boyfriend?"

"Was," Lily said. "He *was* my boyfriend."

And all at once the lyrics she needed to express her sadness, her frustration, and her depression appeared in her mind.

"We should probably write this down," she said, her fingers picking out a tune.

"I'm recording," Vi said, holding up her phone.

"All right." Lily played through several more notes, then opened her mouth to sing, at home here with her sisters, with this guitar in her lap, with songs streaming from her.

She felt comfortable here in Nashville.

But she still wanted to be with Beau.

"When he was my boyfriend," she started, the words coming out slowly in the middle of her range. "The sky shone the deepest blue. The wind hummed a merry tune. When he was my boyfriend...."

"Oh, chicken and biscuits," Vi said, and Lily cut off the next part. She looked at Rose and then Lily, her eyes wide.

"What?" Lily and Rose asked in tandem.

"She's in love with him." Vi giggled and clapped, her glee almost sending Lily into a rage.

"That's not true," she said quickly, glancing at Rose as if her younger sister would be able to tell if Lily loved Beau just by looking at her.

Did she love Beau?

Of course she did.

The guitar thunked on the ground as she let it slip from her grasp. She sucked in a breath, and Rose said, "Oh, my heck. You're in love with him!"

A fresh set of tears pricked her eyes, but Lily was so sick of crying. "So what if I am? It doesn't change anything."

"Oh, honey, of course it does." Vi tapped on her phone a few times, hopefully to stop the recording, and got up. She took the guitar from Lily and set it aside so she could put her arm around Lily's shoulders.

"All right," she said. "Songs later. Tell us how you're going to make up with Beau."

Lily blinked at her. "I'm—what? You think I should make up with him?"

"Of course, silly," Rose said. "If you love him, you should be with him."

"He lives in Wyoming. You guys know that right? It's like, two thousand miles from here."

"Does he love you too?" Vi asked, which only made Lily's head swim. And then spin. And then sink.

"I don't know," she whispered. He'd said a lot of things, but never those three words. "I left him there." She glanced from one sister to another. "Do you think he could forgive that?"

"Well, you've told us precious little about him," Vi said as if she were the Queen of England. "Do sit a spell and tell us more, and then we'll help you decide."

"I know!" Rose clapped her hands. "You could write him a song." Her eager eyes switched from Lily to Vi. "To make up with him. She needs to write him a love song."

TWENTY-ONE

BEAU STARED at the heaps of boxes he'd brought in from the garage. They held glass balls in an assortment of colors and sizes, but Beau couldn't get himself to even get one out. And hanging enough on the twenty-foot tree to make it look festive? That so wasn't happening.

He turned away from the tree, bypassed the kitchen, and went right on outside. He'd already been down to the stables that morning, but his feet took him there again. Bareback wanted to go riding, but the thick snow made it impossible. The best Beau could do in winters like these was try to keep the outdoor arena clear, but he'd even stopped doing that this year.

So he stroked the horse, unable to even disclose why he'd come again. Somehow the horse knew, and he pressed his nose into Beau's shoulder.

Beau's phone rang, and he wanted to ignore it. Ignore

life. Ignore everything. Instead, he pulled the device from his coat pocket and checked it.

A California number. His heart bobbed to the back of his throat, and he swiped the call on quickly.

"Beau Whittaker," he said in his best lawyer voice, the one he used to use when he had an office on Main Street.

"Hello, Mister Whittaker, this is Hilary Clark from the Los Angeles Civil Court. Are you able to attend a hearing on December twenty-third?"

"This December twenty-third?" Beau turned as if he'd find a calendar hanging on the wall of the barn. "Like, in three days?"

"Yes, sir, we realize it's short notice, but a spot came up on the judge's calendar."

"Absolutely," Beau said, thinking maybe he'd call Eli and just spend the holidays in warmer weather. Skip the tree lighting completely. Ignore his life, like he'd just been hoping he could. "I can be there."

"Excellent, I'll put you on Judge Finley's schedule."

"Does the defendant need to be there?" he asked.

"Not if you have the sworn statements," she said. "Though it could help if she was. It's your call."

"Thank you." Beau listened to a few more details, promised to check his email that would have a message confirming everything, and hung up. He glanced around at the horses, his mind spinning.

"I should tell Lily, shouldn't I?" he asked them.

None of them answered. He closed his eyes and prayed to know what to do, but God apparently wanted Beau to make this decision himself, because he didn't get an answer either way.

Instead of deciding, he went up to the house and booked a flight for the following morning. Packed a bag. Called his mother. Texted Eli—who would be in Colorado to see his wife's mother.

And when Beau boarded the plane the next morning, the Christmas tree at Whiskey Mountain Lodge was still void of a single ornament.

DECEMBER twenty-third dawned bright and beautiful, the sound of ocean waves in the back of Beau's mind. This had not been like any December Beau had ever known, and he wondered why in the world he lived in Wyoming.

He enjoyed a morning stroll down the beach, though the wind was whippy and chilly. After dressing in his best suit and double and then triple checking for the files he needed, he called a car service so he could get to court on time.

He had not called, texted, or emailed Lily about the hearing. He'd win, and then he'd let her know everything was over and done. He'd send a bill and be done with her.

His chest squeezed at the thought, and his heart flopped around like a fish out of water. But he'd do it, because she'd been very clear in her decision. She had also not called, texted, or emailed him since driving out of his life. Fine, she had once, just to let him know that he could send an email to yet another address and she'd be checking it regularly.

Beau spotted Kent as soon as he reached the top of the

stairs. The hallway in front of the hearing rooms and court-rooms was wide and long, but Kent was tall and seemed to have honed in on Beau too.

He approached the man, not an ounce of worry in him. "Good morning, Mister Gulbrandsen," he said, extending his hand.

"You shaved," Kent said by way of greeting, and he ignored the invitation to shake hands.

"Yes," Beau said evenly, noting that Kent had not taken the time to clean up his face that morning. He glanced at the clock, knowing they'd be allowed to enter the room in a couple of minutes. "Some of us do research on the judges we're facing."

He gave Kent a wide smile, clapped the other man on the shoulder, and moved away. He didn't need to be first in the room, but he liked to put on a good show as much as the next lawyer.

When he was allowed entrance, he strode forward and took the table on his left, the judge's right. He opened his briefcase and extracted the three folders he'd brought, mentally reviewing the pages and notes he had inside each one. He had them memorized because he'd gone over them so much, but still a flurry of nerves made their way through his stomach.

At the table across the aisle, Kent sat alone, no lawyer present, a single file in front of him. He shifted and glanced at Beau several times, but Beau did not show a single sign of nerves or even so much as give Kent the satisfaction of looking at him.

He did not sit, so he didn't have to spring to his feet

when the deputy came out from a door behind the stand and announced Judge Finley. Beau smiled at the man, received his acknowledgement, and then sat down.

"Mister, uh, Gulbrandsen." The judge looked up from his paperwork, his glasses perched on the end of his nose. "Why do you think you should get additional royalties from the sale of your ex-wife's albums?"

Though his complaint was right in the case, Beau looked at Kent for the answer too, hoping and praying he had a rebuttal for anything the other man came up with.

"Your Honor." Kent stood and buttoned his suit coat jacket. Beau was no fashionista, but he knew an expensive suit when he saw one. After all, Graham and Andrew spent thousands on their suits, and until this past year, so had Beau.

And Kent's suit had easily cost him at least two grand.

"During the time I was married to Lily Everett, she wrote, recorded, and released two albums. I feel I have a part in the construction of those albums as I supported her during that time. Therefore, I feel like I should be monetarily compensated through the royalties those albums continue to accrue."

Accrue. Beau almost scoffed.

"Your Honor." Beau stood but left his jacket unbuttoned. "Miss Everett already paid a lump sum to ensure that Mister Gulbrandsen would not be able to fleece her for her royalties for years to come. Mister Gulbrandsen signed that document upon the finalization of their divorce, and he was indeed paid the amount agreed upon." He had the paperwork should the judge need it, but he'd filed it with the court too, so Judge Finley should've already seen it.

"And as for the 'support' Mister Gulbrandsen claims, he never did have a job during any of the five years he and Miss Everett were married. So any support he claims to have given her, whether that be emotional or physical or what have you, has been satisfied." Beau stood calmly at his table, waiting for Kent to open the doors so Beau could slam them shut again.

Judge Finley looked back at Kent, but he didn't speak. He moved his feet, clearly unprepared for the hearing. True, they hadn't had much time, but Beau had been preparing for this hearing for months.

"It has been difficult to get work," Kent tried, and Beau flipped open one of his folders.

"And yet, the suit Mister Gulbrandsen is wearing in the court today was purchased eight days ago, at Levingston's, a premier men's wear shop here in Los Angeles." Beau held up the single sheet of paper that had come through in his email yesterday morning. "And it was paid for with cash, in the amount of two thousand, two hundred thirty-four dollars and eighty-one cents."

The judge nodded to the deputy, who came forward to take the paper from Beau. Judge Finley took the paper from his deputy and peered at it. "Mister Gulbrandsen?"

"That was a gift," he said, his voice very much on the side of a lie.

"And yet he can't get his benefactors to help with the necessities of life? Shelter? Food?" Beau had receipts for some of those things too, should it come to that. But for now, he held them back. "He needs more money from a woman who has a restraining order against him? A woman who's already paid him to stay out of her life." He cut a glance at Kent, but didn't allow his gaze to settle on the other man at all.

Beau let his words hang in the air, debating if he should play all his cards now and get this hearing over with. He wasn't exactly sure what else Kent would try to pull, though, so Beau waited.

"My parents can't pay for everything," Kent said.

"Then get a job," Beau said.

"Work is extraordinarily difficult to find," the other man spat out.

"Is it?" Beau flipped open his other folder. "I have a sworn statement from Benajamin Buchanan at Valley Pets, who offered you a full time job, with benefits, here. It says that Mister Gulbrandsen was hired on a Thursday in mid-November and was supposed to show up to work on Monday morning. He didn't. Benjamin never heard nor saw him again."

Beau held the paper out as the deputy came forward again. "Keeping a job is probably extraordinarily hard to do when one doesn't show up, I'll give him that."

The judge examined the new paper Beau had presented, and just when Beau thought he might be finished, he launched into what he hoped was his closing argument.

"It's clear to me, Your Honor, that Mister Gulbrandsen simply wants to continue to live in the lap of luxury—Miss Everett's luxury. He's trying to fleece a celebrity, and he should not be allowed to do so. All of his other attempts at extending his alimony benefits have been declined, and he does not deserve, nor has he earned, another cent of Miss Everett's money."

Judge Finley looked up from the paper about halfway through Beau's soliloquy and looked at Kent. "Any last words before I rule?"

"I—No, Your Honor."

"Very well." He laid the paper on the bench in front of him. "Because of the evidence before me, and the rest of the documents in this case, I hereby rule in favor of the defendant. You've gotten your settlement, Mister Gulbrandsen. I see no reason to have your ex-wife continue to pay you for an extended period of time." He picked up his gavel and pounded it once on the bench. "Thank you."

"Thank you, Your Honor," Beau practically yelled up to the bench. He took his time gathering his papers together so Kent would have time to leave the courtroom first. He had no desire to see or talk to the man again.

A smile formed on his face. He'd won.

But his grin faded just as quickly when he realized he had no one to celebrate with.

BEAU BOARDED a plane on Christmas Eve morning, his attention out the window as they took off and headed for Wyoming. He hated that he didn't have someone to go home to, hated that he'd emailed Lily and hadn't heard back from her, hated as the landscape below came into view and it was all snow and grime and gray skies.

Celia would be at the lodge, cooking up a storm for the family dinner that night. Beau had bought gifts and he'd even wrapped them before he'd left for California. He had not decorated the tree, and the thought of doing it made him angry for a reason he couldn't name.

Oh, yes he could. He knew it was because of Lily and how they'd planned to decorate the tree together.

"You've got to get over her," he muttered to himself as he walked through the busy airport, people completing or beginning the holiday travel. He checked his email when he got to his SUV, but Lily still hadn't responded to his message that he'd won her last case.

Frustration coiled within his chest. "She said she'd check this email address," he said, tossing his phone onto the passenger seat. Why wasn't she checking it? She couldn't say thank you to him for saving her thousands of dollars?

He put the SUV in gear and got going. He'd send her a bill when he got back to the lodge. Be done. Focus on his horses and maybe grow out his beard again.

No matter what, he wouldn't be falling in love with his next client, because he was seriously considering giving up the whole bodyguard lawyer career.

TWENTY-TWO

LILY SHOOK HER HEAD. "I'm not sure about this."

"Too bad," Vi singsonged. "You already have the ticket. Rose is getting the car."

But Lily hadn't packed yet. She'd gone along with writing a love song for Beau. She thought maybe she'd get her song-writing mojo back if she did. Maybe she'd be able to take some of the random lyrics she'd collected over the past year and make them into something new for the meeting with their producers after the New Year.

"What if he won't answer the door?" Lily wrung her hands, the sound of a car door slamming in the distance making her jumpy.

"He will." Vi smiled at her. "You've been here for a couple of weeks, and you're miserable. Go see him."

Lily hadn't even been able to check her email, fearing Beau would've solved her case and she'd have no reason to contact him.

"Maybe I should start with a text," she said as Rose came through the front door.

"Are we going or what? You'll miss your flight."

"I haven't packed," Lily said, earning a glare from Vi and a blank stare from Rose. Then her youngest sister threw her head back and laughed.

"Stop it," Lily said.

"You have a credit card," Rose said, coming over to Lily and linking her arm through Lily's elbow. "You're getting on that flight, and you're going to go talk to this Beau Whittaker."

"I don't know...." Lily resisted walking when Rose started toward the door. She wasn't sure why, but a storm raged in her whole soul.

"You're in love with him," Rose said. "It's actually really cute, but I'm tired of listening to you cry at night."

"I do not cry at night," Lily said, slipping her arm away from Rose. At least she hadn't in the last week or so.

"I don't think you were ever this interested in Kent, and you married him," Vi said, walking ahead of them and opening the door. "I agree with Rose. You're going if I have to stuff you on the plane in the baggage hold."

Lily looked back and forth between her sisters. It had been a beautiful couple of weeks with them, and she did want to meet with the producers and start work on a new album.

"We still need to talk about the schedule," she said. They'd spoken about a lot of things—if Lily could work in Wyoming and just fly to Nashville for important meetings or to record. If they could Skype brainstorming sessions. If her sisters could come to the lodge sometimes.

Of course, all of their if's assumed that Beau would even accept Lily's apology and want to get back together. She wouldn't blame him if he didn't, but her heart wailed at the idea of being without him.

"We can talk anytime." Vi gestured out the door. "You just need to be back for the meeting," she added. "It's January eleventh."

Lily knew when the meeting was. "I should at least take my notebook with the songs in it." She turned back and dashed into the music room, where an assortment of instruments waited for the girls to work their magic.

She grabbed the notebook covered in glow-in-the-dark star stickers from a music stand near the piano and tucked it into her purse. When she returned to the foyer, she grabbed Vi in a tight hug. "Thanks, Vi."

Facing Rose, she said, "All right, Rose. Let's get to the airport."

Her younger sisters both whooped, and Lily couldn't help the warm smile that spread across her face.

Her blood turned icier and icier with every mile and every minute that passed. Before she knew it, her plane was taking off and then touching down, and she had no choice but to get off. She was the last one, and the flight attendant stopped her just before she exited.

"Excuse me," she said in a definite Tennessee drawl. "Are you Lily Everett?"

Lily put on the smile she saved for her fans. "I sure am."

The woman beamed and glanced at her co-worker. "I loved your last album."

"Oh, thank you." Lily grinned at her. "Thank you so much. My sisters will love to hear it." She managed to get off the plane then, and she navigated through the small airport to the car rental.

Only an hour to go, she thought, her stomach doing cartwheels at the thought of coming face-to-face with Beau Whittaker. She'd made this drive once before, and it hadn't been easy then.

But then, he didn't know who she was. Then, she'd held all the power. Then, she hadn't been in love with the bearded cowboy who somehow knew every fact about every case in the country.

She wondered if he'd kept the tree and managed to get it decorated. She thought about what he'd been doing all this time and whether or not he was any closer to closing out her last case.

The miles rolled by under her tires, and before she knew it, she pulled into the parking lot at Whiskey Mountain Lodge. It wasn't so late in the day that all the lights should be on at the lodge, but they were. They lit up the stained glass window from the inside, and Lily smiled at the work she'd done. At the memories she had of this place.

She had no idea what to say to Beau. She probably needed to start with something like, "I'm sorry," and "Will you forgive me?" but she hadn't had a hard conversation like that in a long, long time. Maybe ever.

As she got out of the car and approached the front door, she noted that while there were a lot of lights on inside the lodge, there didn't seem to be any cars in the lot. So Celia and Bree weren't here. Beau still could be, and being alone with him in the huge house didn't settle Lily's nerves.

She climbed the steps, stood in front of the door, and slicked her hands down the front of her thighs. "Now," she whispered to herself. "Do it now."

She rang the doorbell and listened to it chime inside the lodge. But nothing stirred, not even Daisy, and that dog never could sit still when someone came to the lodge.

Lily glanced behind her as if Beau would come walking up that way. Of course he didn't. No one did, and suddenly all this wide open land, holding tons and tons of snow, unsettled her. She couldn't stay out here alone.

Just as she was about to either get in the lodge somehow or return to her car, another vehicle pulled into the lot. Lily's heart fired out extra beats every other second until she realized it was Bree.

She breathed, trying to tame her adrenaline and regulate her pulse. She lifted her hand in greeting to Bree and went down the steps to greet her friend.

"Hey," she said as Bree straightened from the driver's seat.

"Lily." She bounced over to her and held her in a tight hug. "What are you doing here?" She held Lily at arm's length and peered into her eyes.

"I came to...I just wanted to talk to Beau."

Bree dropped her hands and turned back to her car, something strange crossing her face that Lily couldn't get more than a glimpse of. "He's not here right now."

"Oh." Disappointment cut through Lily. "Do you know

when he'll be back?" She could get coffee in town, wait a spell, and then talk to him. She didn't want to go through another night where she hadn't at least spoken to him.

"He's gone to California," she said. "Yesterday morning. He had a hearing today. This morning, actually." She popped the trunk and pointed. "You want to help?"

Lily stepped over to the car, needing answers. If she had to carry in groceries to get them, so be it. "A hearing?" She gathered two paper bags into her arms and made to step with Bree toward the lodge.

"For his last case," Bree said, taking the steps carefully and going through the unlocked front door. "Your case. He's flying home in the morning, just in time for the family dinner." She traipsed through the living room and into the kitchen, Lily right behind her.

"My case?" she repeated. "I haven't heard from him."

"He probably just wanted to wait and see if he'd won or not." Bree wouldn't look directly at her, and Lily realized her sudden departure from Whiskey Mountain Lodge had made life difficult for more than just her and Beau.

"How has he been?" Lily asked as she set her bags on the counter.

Bree did meet her eye then. "He's...about what you would expect." She nodded a few times and headed back for the door.

When Lily passed the Christmas tree this time, she realized that it was not decorated. Christmas Eve was tomorrow. "Bree," she called after the woman. "Are you guys still doing the tree lighting?"

Bree didn't break her stride or look back as she went

down the steps. "I honestly don't know. Beau hasn't called it off, and these are only half of the groceries. Celia's bringing the other half." She exhaled heavily, and Lily got moving to help her bring in all the food from her trunk.

"The tree's not decorated," Lily pointed out, though Bree obviously knew.

"Right."

"You guys won't do it?"

"Beau's been...moody about the tree. Celia and I agreed not to touch it. None of the other brothers come up here, so it'll be interesting to see what happens tomorrow night."

Lily started unpacking the groceries, everything from sour cream and butter, to lentils and coconut oil. "Do you think he'd mind if I decorated the tree? I saw the boxes of ornaments out there."

Bree stopped working. "Are you planning to stay for the holidays then?"

"I was considering it," Lily said coolly. "Unless Beau's already hired another client and my room isn't available."

Bree stepped right in front of her then, a stern look on her face. "Lily." She cleared her throat as her cheeks turned a shade of red Lily had never seen before. "I'm just going to say this, and I mean no disrespect. I like you. It's good to see you. But if you're just going to run right back to Nashville, maybe you should just go now. I don't want to see Beau go through...that again."

"What again?" Lily asked, though she had a very strong suspicion that she knew exactly what Beau had been through since she'd left. And that was her fault.

The lyrics to the love song she'd written for him started

on repeat. "We have some things to work out, sure," she said. "But I don't want to hurt him."

"Sometimes we do things unintentionally," Bree said.

She wasn't wrong, but Lily didn't know how to go back in time and somehow convince her irrational self to stay in Wyoming. She wished that were the case, because then maybe she could've been warned about what leaving Coral Canyon would do to her.

"I'm here to apologize," Lily said. "I don't intend to hurt him, intentionally or otherwise."

"All right." Bree continued putting the groceries away, and Lily slipped into the living room to face the giant Christmas tree she'd helped haul through that skinny doorway. Fine, it was a double-wide door, but it had still been a challenge getting the tree inside the lodge.

She stepped over to a stack of boxes, where six red, blue, and gold balls waited. She opened the package and began adding hooks to the end of each ornament.

The work was tedious and slow, with plenty of second-guessing. Was that ornament in the right spot? Had she put too many silver ones too close together?

After about an hour—and eight boxes later—she stepped back to admire her work. A smile tugged at the corners of her mouth, especially when Bree brought her a steaming cup of coffee.

"Looks good," Bree said as she stood at Lily's side. She nudged her with her hip. "And your room is still open if you want to bring in your bag."

"I don't have one," Lily said, yanking her phone out of

her pocket to check the time. "I better get down into town to get a few things before everything closes."

And after that, she just needed to practice the song she'd written for Beau and find the right words to apologize to him.

TWENTY-THREE

"NO, I DON'T NEED A RIDE," Beau's mother said, and disappointment cut through him. He'd stopped by her house to see if she wanted to come up to the lodge with him, but she was steadfastly refusing.

And Beau didn't want to go up to that huge house all by himself. Yes, Bree and Celia would already be there. The stockings were probably hung, and the whole place probably smelled like salty ham and buttery potatoes. He usually loved the picture-perfect atmosphere of the lodge, but this year he didn't want to deal with any of it.

"You sure?" he asked for the second time, watching his mother as she flitted around the kitchen.

"Yes. Jason and I are coming up later." She flashed him a smile, but she wouldn't look directly at him.

"Mom, what am I missing?"

"Nothing. I just want to wait for Jason. He has to work today."

"I thought he was retired."

"He is, but he helps out at the hardware store a few days a week, and they close today at three. We'll be up after that."

As it was only noon, and Beau couldn't just hang around his mom's place for that long—he had a Christmas tree to decorate, after all—he stood up. Exhaling hard, like his mother was putting him out, he said, "All right. See you up there."

She waved at him a bit too enthusiastically. "You too. Congrats on your case."

"Thanks." He walked out and got behind the wheel, his dread about returning to the lodge almost suffocating him.

"Just go," he told himself. He had to at least put some lights on the tree, as well as hang as many ornaments as he could. So he pointed his SUV toward the lodge and made it there in record time.

Two cars sat in the parking lot, and he eased past them and into the garage around the side of the lodge. He collected his bag and entered the house, a heaviness settling onto his shoulders he hadn't expected.

The scent hanging in the air was one part sugar, one part meat, and one part pine tree. Holiday music blasted through the wired-in stereo system, and he didn't wholly hate it. So maybe he had some Christmas spirit left.

He wheeled his bag down the hall, stopping in the kitchen long enough to say, "Hey, ladies. I'm home."

Both Bree and Celia looked up, alarm on their faces. "Beau," Celia said as if she hadn't expected to see him for days yet. Bree scrambled to turn down the music while Celia bustled around the counter. She glanced behind him, and Beau did too. But there was nothing there.

"What's going on?" he asked, facing her again.

"Nothing."

It was the second time someone had said that to him today, and he was growing tired of the fibs. "Right. I'm going to go shower."

Bree appeared in the other doorway that led into the kitchen, farther down the hall. "Uh, you might want to check on the...." She nodded toward the living room.

Beau groaned. "I know I said I'd do the tree. I just...." *Can't.* He didn't want to decorate it without Lily. His heart squirmed in his chest painfully, and he sighed.

"How are we supposed to have a tree lighting without the lights?" Celia asked. "On the *tree?*"

"Honestly, I'm surprised you two didn't do it while I was gone." He took a step down the hall, still deciding if he had the stamina to face the tree and all those ornament boxes he'd brought in days ago.

"Well, we didn't," Celia said. "And think of Bailey. She'll be so disappointed if the tree isn't decorated."

Was it Beau's imagination or was Celia practically yelling?

"Fine," he said. "Let me go put my bag away, and I'll—" His words failed him as he arrived at the doorway to the living room and looked in.

"Lily."

She stood there, wearing a bright red, festive Christmas sweater that hugged her curves in all the right ways. She wore jeans and big, puffy socks, her nearly white hair spilling over her shoulders.

He blinked, sure he was hallucinating. Maybe it was the flying. The time change. The depression. But when he looked again, she still stood there.

"I started decorating the tree," she said, her voice just as wonderful and musical as he remembered. "I hope you're not upset."

"Upset?" he echoed stupidly. He took in the tree, noting that the whole thing was almost finished, even the branches at the top.

"Yeah, Bree said you wanted to do it." Lily tucked her hands into her back pockets, worry zipping around in her expression.

"Well, Bree lied."

"Hey," Bree protested behind him.

Beau chuckled and left his bag in the hallway, taking a daring step into the living room, closer to Lily. "What are you doing here?"

"I miss you," she blurted. "And I'm sorry, and I wanted to come back as soon as I left, but I didn't know how, and—you shaved."

Beau reached up and ran his hand along his mostly clean-shaven jaw. "Yeah, I had to go to court."

"I got the email this morning. Celia convinced me not to reply."

"She did, huh?" Beau didn't look behind him, though he knew Celia and Bree were standing there watching.

"Thank you for winning all of my cases, Beau."

Oh, she couldn't say his name. Not like that. Not like she cared about him and wanted to be with him for the holidays. It wasn't fair. He couldn't get his heart shattered again.

"Is that why you came? To say thank you?"

"No." She took a step toward him, and then rocked back. "I came to sing you a song."

Surprise made Beau lift his eyebrows. Sure, he knew Lily was a singer and a songwriter, but she sure hadn't done a lot of it over the few months she'd lived at the lodge.

Bree ducked past him and handed a guitar to Lily. She perched on the edge of the couch, the Christmas tree beside her making the perfect holiday image for a country music postcard. Beau's heart beat in his chest like hummingbird wings while Lily tuned the guitar and then looked up at him.

"My sisters helped me write it," she said, her voice a bit on the quiet side. "They'll be here in time for the tree lighting."

Beau nodded, sure his own vocal chords wouldn't work right now. Lily had simply walked back into her life here. Not only that, but she'd taken over of some things, like the tree decorating and lighting, and she'd invited her sisters to share the lodge's traditions.

Not the lodge, he thought as Lily started plucking the strings. *The Whittaker family traditions.*

"When he was my boyfriend," she started, her tone matching the guitar's perfectly. Lily really was so talented.

"The sky shone the deepest blue. The wind hummed a merry tune. When he was my boyfriend." She looked right at him, her eyes earnest as she sang about how happy she'd been when he was her boyfriend.

The song took a turn in the middle, toward finding her own way, and then she sang, "So when I go back, I hope he'll forgive me. I hope he'll see I love him. I hope, hope, hope, that he'll be my boyfriend again."

Her fingers moved along the guitar strings effortlessly for a few more seconds, playing out the last notes of the song.

She finished and stood, her eyes shining with tears, and Beau swept toward her and gathered her right into his arms, where he always wanted her to be.

"I love you too," he whispered into her hair as they swayed, as her shoulders shook and she cried. "Shh, now, it's all right. I love you too."

But he felt like crying too. He'd never imagined that he'd find Lily in his house when he got here. If he'd known, he wouldn't have stopped by his mother's and tried to get her to come up to the lodge with him.

He'd have driven as fast and as straight as he could. He heard sniffling behind him, and he turned to find both Bree and Celia wiping their eyes, and he smiled at them. "I suppose you all think this is just wonderful."

"It is," Bree said, her voice a bit throaty.

"Pat's coming to dinner," Celia blurted. "Will you please be nice to him?"

"Pat Rusk?" Beau asked, tucking Lily against his side as she wiped her tears too. "Of course I'll be nice to him. I'm nice to everyone."

Celia nodded and sniffed and said, "I'm sure I'm letting something burn." She scampered out of the living room, and Bree went a moment later too.

Beau surveyed the Christmas tree, impressed with how much Lily had done. "When did you get here?" he asked.

"Yesterday about lunchtime," she said, gazing up at him.

"I really am sorry. I...I don't know what happened. I was scared, I suppose. I thought maybe I did want my recording life back."

"And do you?" Because she was a gorgeous singer, and if she wanted to write songs and perform all over the world, Beau thought he'd just buy an RV and follow her around.

"Yes and no," she said. "Vi, Rose, and I want to keep writing songs, but we've talked a lot about me living here and using technology to collaborate and communicate. We think it'll work."

He nodded and reached out to straighten a blue ornament that looked crooked.

"I'll have to go to Nashville sometimes," she said. "But once the recording starts, it honestly doesn't take that long."

"And touring?" Beau honestly wanted to know, but his heart was terrified of the answer.

"I'm not going to tour. I've already told Vi and Rose, and we've let Shawn, our manager, know as well. He'll be talking to the producers about that."

"No tours," Beau whispered. "Are you sure, Lily?"

"It's three hundred days on the road," she said. "I might have enjoyed it before, but I was kind of hoping to put that time toward learning to ride a horse, and maybe having a baby...."

Beau let her words sink right down deep into his soul. "A baby?" He turned and looked at her then and found hope and happiness shining in her face.

She shrugged. "Yeah, I mean, I think I could be a decent enough mom, and I think I've finally found a man I want to have a family with."

He blinked at her, a bit flabbergasted.

"It's you, by the way," she said with a giggle. She reached up and ran her fingertips along his jaw to his ear. "I would like the beard back, though."

"Oh, you would, huh?" Beau grinned at her, the strength of his feelings almost making him sink to his knees. Relief that she'd come back. Gratitude that the Lord had given her what she needed, but also allowed her to return to him.

"I like the mountain man look."

"Hmm." He leaned down and touched his nose to the tip of hers. "Can I kiss you without the beard?"

"I suppose."

So he did, and it was just as magical and magnificent as the first time, the love he felt between them swirling and solidifying into something he knew he'd never be able to deny.

TWENTY-FOUR

LILY SHOULD NEVER HAVE DOUBTED that Beau would forgive her and take her back. The man really was a great big teddy bear, although kissing him without a beard was definitely a new experience.

She broke their kiss and drew in a deep breath of his woodsy cologne, the pure male smell of him. "So you had to go to California for court?" she asked.

"Yep. But it was a fast hearing, and wow, the ocean is beautiful even in December." He glanced around the living room, with all of its beautiful, raw wood, those high-as-the-sky ceilings, and the stained glass window. "Wyoming is so...gray."

Lily laughed and kept her arms wrapped tightly around him. "You have money, Beau. Why don't you travel?"

"I've never thought about it, I guess."

"Well, instead of me touring, we should travel the world."

Beau smiled down at her, pure love shining in those dark, gorgeous eyes. "I'd like that."

"Now." She exhaled and stepped out of his arms. "The Christmas tree. Do you think it's ready?"

He turned to face it, really taking his time to examine every branch. "I think so. Are you going to do the lighting?"

A blip of fear stole through Lily. "I—doesn't a family member do that?"

"Not always," he said, though it was clear he wasn't really telling the truth. "I'll talk a little and welcome people. Then we light the tree and pass out gifts. It's informal, really."

Lily scoffed and shook her head. "It is not, and you know it. I can't *believe* you hadn't even put up one ornament."

"I...couldn't," he said. "It was too painful."

"Why's that?"

"We were supposed to do it together."

Lily heard all the emotion in Beau's voice, and another round of guilt struck her right behind the ribs. "I know. And then I did it all alone."

"Not quite." He stepped away from her and picked up a box she hadn't seen around the side of the tree. "There are four left."

She smiled and hugged herself as he hung the silver ornaments on the tree, even directing him to a bald patch several feet up on one side.

"I'm starving," he said.

Lily laughed. "Yeah, you really worked up an appetite putting on those few ornaments."

"Let's go see what Celia will let us steal from the kitchen."

"Oh, you'll get nothing there," Lily said. "She sent me down for sandwiches for dinner last night."

"Really?" Beau stepped into the kitchen, where the holiday music was once again blasting through the speakers. Lily watched him walk over to Celia, and the man must really possess words of magic, because she tipped her head back and laughed, then went to the fridge and pulled out a container of something.

Beau motioned for Lily to join them, and she did so reluctantly. She liked watching him from afar, witnessing his warm spirit and how he seemed to genuinely like everyone. And they all liked him too.

"Ham and split pea soup," he said. "It's delicious."

"I didn't realize grown ups ate this," she said. "This looks like what my grandmother would feed us as girls."

"It's so good," Beau said, accepting the plastic container from Celia and moving over to the microwave himself.

"Can I have toast with mine?" she asked. "Gramma always let me have toast." Her last two words echoed through the kitchen when the Christmas song that had been playing suddenly ended.

Beau looked at her and then Celia, and right as *Jingle Bells* came on, he started laughing. Celia too, and Lily couldn't help but join in. Oh, how she loved this place, and these people. And she knew that she had been led here by a higher power, and that she had absolutely made the right decision in returning to Wyoming to spend Christmas in Coral Canyon.

When Beau stopped laughing, Lily joined him in front of the microwave. "Can I go to church with you now?" she asked.

He bent, got a loaf of bread out of a nearby drawer, and handed it to her. His expression radiated joy when he said, "I sure would like that."

"THIS IS VI," Lily said, indicating her sister with the short hair. "And Rose. My sisters." She beamed at them, glad she'd been able to make the drive to Jackson Hole to pick them up. Well, Beau had driven. And once he'd pulled over so he could kiss her on the side of the road. But they had picked up her sisters at the airport and brought them back to the lodge.

Beau's mom grinned for all she was worth. "The Everett Sisters. Lily. Vi. Rose. It's so good to have you here." She hugged them all, and Lily was glad she'd warned her sisters about the hugging.

"And my grandparents. Stu and Thea." She put her arm around Pops and started naming off the members of Beau's family, as well as Celia and Bree. At least Pat, Celia's boyfriend, looked like he'd been hit with a cement block too.

Rose and Vi blended into the crowd effortlessly, having played the social scene for years. They were much better than Lily at it, actually, and she stuck closer to her grandparents before finally passing them off to Amanda and Jason as a conversation about the black bears in Yellowstone began.

"Last call for gifts in the stockings," Laney yelled, and Lily ducked out of the room. She hadn't come completely unprepared, but in the safety of her bedroom, she found the idea of slipping cash into the stockings quite ridiculous.

But she didn't have anything else, and she didn't want to skip this tradition. Beau had assured her that gifts were optional, but Lily knew that wasn't really true.

As she pulled out the money envelope from the bank, someone tapped on her door. Vi ducked inside a moment later, saying, "Rose went to get the CDs. We need to sign them fast. Do you have any wrapping paper?"

"CDs?" Lily asked.

"Yeah, we brought our latest album for everyone." Vi cocked her head. "Did you forget? Rose said she'd bring them. We just need to sign them, and wrap them, and get them in the stockings."

"I don't know if we have time for that." Lily stepped toward the door. "Let me go ask Beau what time he's planning on the—oof." She caught the door before it could do too much damage to her body and backed up as Rose entered with a big box in her arms.

"We don't have time to wrap," she said between puffs of breath. "Graham—I think it was Graham? He's the one with kids, right? Anyway, he just said five minutes until the tree lighting."

She dumped the CDs on the bed, and Lily's panic bloomed. Maybe she'd be giving out those twenties.

"So let's sign quick," Vi said. "We can do that." She opened the box and pulled out a few permanent markers. "I want the gold." She handed Lily silver, and Rose took bronze.

Five minutes later, they had quite the stack of signed CDs, and Beau knocked on the door. "Lily?"

"Ready?" she asked her sisters.

"Ready," Rose said, finishing her name with a flourish.

Lily opened the door and said, "We just need to put these in the stockings, okay?"

"All right. Want me to carry them?"

"Yes, please." Lily stood back and let Beau pick up the box off the bed. She waited until her sisters had followed him out, then she grabbed her money envelope again and scurried down the hall to the living room.

People milled about, but no one really paid attention to the stockings. So adding the CDs, even though they were unwrapped, worked out fine. Lily slipped cash into the kids' stockings, as well as some for Bree and Celia, who had helped her so much while she'd been here the past few months.

Then she joined Beau as he stood beside the fireplace. "Welcome, everyone," he said in a booming voice that lifted right up to the rafters. "And Merry Christmas."

Choruses of "Merry Christmas" came back to him, and he grinned around the room. "Is everyone here? Did Celia come in from the kitchen?"

"Right here," she said from her perch on the steps leading to the second floor.

"All right," he said. "Welcome to Whiskey Mountain Lodge for our fourth Christmas together." He paused for a moment, his hand searching for Lily's. Once he found it and latched onto her, he continued with, "I love this tradition. We're going to light the tree, and then we'll take down our stockings, and then Celia has dinner in the dining room."

He surveyed the crowd again, and Lily felt every eye on her too. She shifted a bit before finally catching Vi's gaze.

Her sister looked happy, a smile on her face, and she nodded a little at Lily.

"Let's see," Beau said. "I didn't think through who was going to light the tree this year."

"Have Lily do it," Graham called out, and heat shot to Lily's face. If everyone wasn't staring at her before, they certainly were now.

"Lily?" Beau looked at her. "You want to?"

"I don't know how," she said.

"It's a switch," Beau told her. "You just push it." He indicated a bank of light switches on the wall that separated the living room from the hallway and the kitchen. "Right there."

Lily released his hand and stepped over to the other wall. "Okay, ready?" For some reason, her heart seemed to be bobbing in her chest when it should've been beating.

Beau nodded, and Lily flipped the switch up. The lights came on, all white and lovely and reflecting off the ornaments. People oohed and ahhed, and Lily stood there and felt absolute joy. Peace. And love.

Beau tucked her into his side, and Lily sighed as she gazed at the tree they had decorated together. Hopefully it would be the first of many, right here in this lodge.

"Before the stockings get passed out," Andrew said, standing. "We have some news we'd like to share." He gripped his wife's hand, and Becca stood too.

They both grinned at the crowd and Becca finally said. "Oh, you want me to say it? You're the one who writes all the speeches."

People laughed, and Lily watched them interact with such love and adoration for each other.

"Fine, I'll do it." Andrew pressed a kiss to her temple. "Becca's pregnant. We're going to have a baby!"

Amanda launched herself off the couch, a squeal filling the living room. She grabbed onto Becca, and then Andrew, and there were a few minutes of congratulations and celebration. Lily had never particularly wanted children—until she'd met Beau. Now, it seemed that was all she could think about.

"Help me pass out the stockings?" His breath tickled her ear his mouth was so close, and Lily almost jumped. She did shiver, and then she nodded. She took stockings to people, and then accepted hers from Beau.

"Mom, I got money!" Bailey yelled, and Lily paused to watch the reaction.

"That's great, Bay," Laney said, seemingly undisturbed by the gift. "Oh my goodness." Her hand fluttered around her throat and she glanced up at Lily. "You guys signed these." She held up her CD. "Signed by all three sisters!"

Lily grinned at her, and she left her stocking on the hearth so she could stand with Vi and Rose and Laney and get her picture taken. That set off quite the round of picture-taking, and she heard people saying things like, "We've never had a celebrity at our Christmas Eve dinner," and "Who knew they'd be so nice?"

By the time she got back to her stocking, it had disappeared. She glanced around for it, and someone said, "Hey, over here," in a really bad stage whisper.

She found Beau holding her stocking and standing in the hall, and she walked over to him. "Holding that hostage?"

"Kind of, yeah." He glanced into the living room, which still seemed abuzz with the activities of pulling treats and small packages out of stockings. "Can I talk to you alone for a minute?"

"Sure." She followed him down the hall to his bedroom, which she had never actually stepped foot in before. Now she did, and he pushed the door closed behind them.

He swallowed and then cleared his throat, and that kept Lily's attention on him instead of taking in what this master bedroom looked like. "You're kind of freaking me out," she said.

"I'm kind of freaking out, because I'm not sure you're ready for this, and I might die if you say no."

Lily's own heart seemed to be in a dead sprint for some unknown finish line. "Are you going to ask me to marry you?"

"You're ruining it."

"Because I was actually going to talk to you about that...."

Beau shook his head, his eyes taking on an electric edge she'd only seen a few times—when he was agitated or angry. "No. No *way* are you asking me to marry you." He dropped to both knees. "I don't have a ring, but I'm madly in love with you, and I want to make your life as wonderful and joyous as this day has been."

He paused to take a breath, and Lily couldn't help herself. She opened her mouth and they said together, "Will you marry me?"

Beau shook his head though he was smiling, and laughed.

Lily knelt in front of him too, and took his handsome face in both of her hands. "I will, if you grow the beard back for the ceremony."

"Done," he said.

"Done," she repeated, and then she kissed her fiancé.

TWENTY-FIVE

THE FOLLOWING CHRISTMAS

"Are you sure, Mom?" Beau stood in the airport with his mother, searching the crowd for his brother Eli. Or Meg. Or his nephew Stockton. They were supposed to be on this flight, but it felt like two hundred people had walked by and there was still no sign of them.

"He said flight seventy-four-fifty. It should be here." She looked at her phone, but Beau knew she was less than reliable when it came to using technology. He scanned the crowd one more time, and then pulled out his own phone. He swiped and typed, scrolled and tapped before learning that flight seventy-four-fifty had been delayed for over forty-five minutes leaving Denver.

"They're late," he said. "Let's go sit down again." He was glad he hadn't brought Lily, as she had a million-plus-one things to do for their wedding the day after Christmas, and they still had to decorate the tree for the Christmas Eve dinner the following night. Beau wasn't sure why they hadn't done it earlier, other than it now felt like a new, private tradition of their own to save the decorating for the morning of Christmas Eve.

Lily's sisters and parents had arrived a few days ago, and all the Everetts were in prep mode for what would likely be the biggest event Coral Canyon had ever seen. Maybe even the whole state of Wyoming.

Beau hadn't wanted anything grand, but Lily had, and he'd let her do what she wanted. As long as she showed up and walked down the aisle, said "I do," when it was time, and became his wife, he didn't care what else happened. They could have salmon or bison or beef. He didn't care. She could have daisies or roses or lilies. He didn't care.

He just wanted her to be his wife so badly, and his impatience for that event bled over into everything these days—including waiting for his brother's delayed flight.

He hadn't seen Eli in a while—since he'd come in June when Becca had had her baby. Meg and Stockton had stayed for about a month, but Eli had only come for a week.

Beau's leg bounced while he waited, and what felt like forever later but was probably only twenty minutes, his mom said, "Oh, he just texted. They just landed."

"Great." Beau stood up, though it would probably take another several minutes for his brother to get off the plane and make their way out of the airport. They'd need to pick up their bags, but at least they'd pass security before then.

Sure enough, another ten minutes went by before he saw his brother bobbing through the crowd. "There he is." He wasn't sure why he was so excited to see Eli, other than they'd been close growing up, and Beau wanted Eli there for Christmas and the wedding.

He bent down, and then Stockton came shooting through the people. Beau laughed as he scooped his nephew up, groaning. "Holy cow, boy. You've gotten heavy."

"I'm nine years old now," he said, his smile full of odd adult teeth mixed with baby ones.

"Wow, you're ancient," Beau said, setting him back on his feet. "What took you guys so long?"

"They wouldn't let the plane take off. Something about de-icing the wings."

Eli showed up, his grin just as wide as Beau's. He grabbed onto him and clapped him on the back. "Finally doing it. Finally getting married," Eli said.

"Yep." Beau pulled back and beamed at him as Meg arrived, carrying a little girl with skin as dark as coffee. Beau's heart swelled until he thought it would burst. "You got her." He looked into the little girl's eyes, wonder and joy and love coursing through him.

"Why didn't you tell us?" His mother reached for the girl, and Meg passed her over.

"This is Averie," she said. "We've only had her a couple of weeks, and Eli thought it would be a nice surprise." She linked her arm through his. "He was very worried about overshadowing the wedding, so he didn't want to say anything."

Beau's mom ran her hands over Averie's head and grinned at her. "Well, aren't you the cutest thing ever? How old is she?"

"She just turned three," Meg said, also beaming at the

child. "She seems to be doing quite well." She swiped quickly at her eyes, and her smile was a bit wobbly when she met Beau's gaze.

"Oh, come on," he said, gathering her into his arms and holding her while she sniffled. "I'm so glad you got her, Meg. She deserves to overshadow the wedding."

"Don't say that in front of Lily," Eli said with a chuckle. "All right. Let's get our bags and get out of here. I've had enough of airports today."

THE MORNING of Beau's wedding dawned with rays of sunlight coming in the office windows. He'd been up for hours, his excitement preventing him from sleeping. He'd been praying for a solid month that there would be good weather on December twenty-sixth, if only so he and Lily could catch their flight to Paris.

It was a city Lily had always wanted to visit and never had —which was quite a feat, as Beau had learned as he'd tried to plan the perfect honeymoon.

They were spending three weeks in Europe, and Beau had spent long hours reviewing the itineraries, booking flights and B&B's and making sure everything was going to be perfect for the next twenty-one days.

"You're working?" Lily's voice interrupted him, and he glanced away from the window.

"Obviously, I'm staring outside, marveling at why a woman like you has stuck around this long."

"Mm." She slipped one hand between his body and his

arm, and latched onto it with the other. "Must be because of the horses."

"Which you still haven't ridden."

"Okay, then, the part-time chef."

"You're as good as Celia now."

"Fine, it must be because of the cowboy that lives in this lodge." She tilted her head back and smiled at him, and Beau leaned down to kiss her.

"I love you," he whispered.

"I'm so glad the beard is back," she said with a giggle. "Now, go on. You better get your stuff together. We have to leave in thirty minutes."

"It's ready." He returned his attention out the window.

"Are you sure?" Lily asked, and that brought Beau's eyes back to hers.

"Oh, boy," he said when he saw that coy smile on her mouth. "What have you done this time?" She'd spent the last twelve months making him the happiest man on the planet. He had not taken on another client, but he'd worked with her on her songs, and flew to Nashville with her when she needed to go, and took care of his beloved horses.

She'd spent time in the kitchen, learning to cook. And out with the horses, just talking to them in the pastures. And writing songs and recording an album.

"It's nothing, really," she said, though Beau had learned that all of Lily's surprises were something. Usually something that had taken her weeks or a month to prepare to give him, like the stained glass window.

"And it's really a token of peace, because I'm about to ask you for a huge favor."

Beau twisted toward her. "Oh? What is it?"

"Go check your room first."

He squinted at her and then walked out of the office, knowing she'd follow him. She never could let him open one of her surprises in private. Just inside his bedroom door, his garment bag with his tux was still draped over his bag, so that hadn't changed. He *was* packed and ready to go over to the church where they would be married.

But now a bright red package sat on top of the garment bag. It wasn't a terribly large box, but definitely more substantial than a set of cufflinks. He picked it up, surprised it weighed so little.

"What is this?" he asked, somewhat nervous now.

"Just open it."

He did, ripping right into the paper and finding a box about the same size as a manila folder. Inside, there was only one sheet of paper, along with a bookmark with a horse's hoofprint on it.

He scanned the paper, reading quickly, and then exclaiming, "You bought me a horse?"

Lily grinned and shrugged. "Seemed like a good wedding present for a cowboy."

Desire dove through Beau. She knew him so well, and he loved her so much. He kissed her again, really taking his time to let her know what he couldn't wait for once they left Coral Canyon.

"So," he said, his mouth still only a breath from hers. "What's the favor?" He kissed her again before she could answer, and he suspected it might be something he didn't want to do when she carried on for so long.

He finally pulled away and said, "Lily."

"Vi wants to make a change in her life. She's struggling, Beau, really struggling."

"Yeah, I know. You've told me all about it. Bob still being an idiot?"

"She broke up with Bob," she said. "At least in her mind. He hasn't seemed to have gotten the memo."

"Oh, one of those."

"Yeah, one of those."

Beau waited, because the favor still hadn't come out yet.

"So I told her she should move here. Hire you."

Beau blinked, surprise flowing freely from head to toe. "But I'm not doing the lawyer thing anymore." He rubbed the beard. "Mountain man, remember? Horse trainer."

"Oh, please. You're in that office by five AM every morning. You can handle a simple stalking case."

Beau cocked his head. "And?"

"And I might have told her the whole basement was open and she should move in here."

Beau fell back a step. "She's going to move in with us?"

She picked up the paper with the quarterhorse's breeding and name on it. "I bought you a horse to keep you busy."

"I don't want a horse to keep me busy." Beau stared at her and put both of his hands on her waist. "I want *you* to keep me busy."

Lily laughed, a beautiful sound that made Beau chuckle too.

"You won't even know she's here," Lily said.

"Nice try."

"I won't spend all my time with her," she said next.

"Right. I believe that." Beau sighed and looked away. "I just want...I love you. I want us to rely on each other. I'm not saying you'll run to her to talk things out, but it's just...."

"I won't," she said. "And she can't come until she finishes with the record anyway, and that's not until March. Maybe April."

So they'd have a few months alone together in the lodge. "I don't know," he said.

"She can buy something," Lily said. "I just—she's really struggling, you know?"

He did know. He didn't want to be a selfish brother-in-law. "I know. It's fine. Thank you for the horse." He took the paper back and looked at the name. "But we have to rename this thing. No horse should be called Clyde for his whole life."

He hoped Lily would laugh, but she didn't. He honestly hadn't expected her to.

"Really?" she asked, and he knew she didn't mean the horse's name couldn't be Clyde—though it absolutely could not.

"Really, Lily." He kissed her again. "I love you, and if your sister needs to be here for a bit, it's fine."

"Maybe things will be better in a few months, and she won't have to move in here."

"Maybe." He picked up his garment bag. "Now, let's go get married." He'd just latched onto his other bag with all his toiletries when her hand came down on his.

"I love you, Beau."

"Love you too."

HER COWBOY BILLIONAIRE BODYGUARD   227

Lily didn't let go of his hand quite yet. "I want you to keep me busy too."

"Oh, I'm planning on it, sweetheart," he said with a grin. "Now, come on. We can't miss our own wedding."

Beau and Lily made things work! I'm so happy! If you are too, **please leave a review now**.

Join Liz's List and never miss a new release or a special sale on her books.

Read on for a sneak peek at HER COWBOY BILLIONAIRE BULL RIDER, featuring Lily's sister, Vi, and the man who comes to the lodge after having retired from winning bull riding championships. **Then go preorder it!**

SNEAK PEEK! HER COWBOY BILLIONAIRE BULL RIDER CHAPTER ONE

TODD CHRISTOPHERSON GOT out of his huge tour bus, deciding on the spot that he should've been paying his driver a lot more to get him all over the country to compete in professional rodeo events.

This bus was *huge*, and Todd hadn't had the easiest time getting it down the narrow canyon and into the valley town of Coral Canyon, where he was born and raised.

He took in a deep breath of the mountain air, glad to be back in a familiar place. A punch of loneliness hit him when he remembered he couldn't get in the truck behind the bus and go visit his parents. They were still on-tour with Taylor, Todd's brother, and they'd sold their house here in Coral Canyon when his sister had moved to Grand Junction. Years ago.

Todd hadn't had a permanent home in almost two decades, and as he gazed at the Tetons above him, he knew it was time to change that.

Which is why you retired, he told himself. He fished in his pocket for his keys and headed to the back of the bus to unhook the truck he'd been towing. He'd be able to stay at the RV park for as long as he wanted, and the tour bus really had everything he needed—but it was on wheels.

Todd didn't want to get rid of the bus, but he thought he was ready for more stable walls. And to do that, he needed to find a realtor. And lucky for him, he knew his cousin, Collin, happened to be one of those—and he still lived in Coral Canyon.

So twenty minutes later, Todd pulled into the office building where his cousin worked, and before he'd made it to the front door, Collin came out, a huge smile on his face.

"Well, if it isn't six-time world champion Todd Christopherson!" He spoke in a rodeo announcer voice, like Todd would be flying out of the gate on a bull named Two-Timer at any moment.

Todd couldn't help chuckling and shaking his head. "How are you, Collin?"

"You know they're putting up a billboard with your face on it, right?" They shook hands, and Collin gestured him into the building.

"Who's 'they'?" Todd asked, mildly horrified. Though it wouldn't be the first time he'd seen his face on a billboard, he certainly wasn't advertising an upcoming event in Coral Canyon. He'd done plenty of photo shoots and promo spots for the rodeo in the various cities where he rode. More tickets sold meant more money for everyone, himself included.

"The town council," Collin said. "It got final approval at last week's meeting. Everyone is buzzing about when you'll roll into town."

"Well, that happened a couple of hours ago." Todd followed Collin into his office. As far as he knew, nothing had changed. He didn't need a parade. The air was still made of oxygen, and the sun sky ruled the sky.

Todd Christopherson couldn't change any of that.

"So you need someplace to live?" Collin asked as he sat behind his desk.

"Yeah," Todd said.

"I think we can do that." Collin tapped on his keyboard. "Let's start with your wish list."

Todd blinked and tried to think through what a normal person's wishlist would be. "I'd like a backyard," he said slowly.

Collin burst into laughter, but Todd wasn't sure what he'd said that was so funny. When he didn't chuckle along with his cousin, Collin quieted. He cleared his throat. "Todd, all the houses here have backyards. What size are you thinking?"

"Something big enough for a dog, maybe."

"Sure, sure," Collin said. "Keep going. Number of bedrooms? Mountain view? In a neighborhood? With horse land and water rights?" He looked at Todd. "What are you thinking?"

Todd had obviously not been thinking enough. He didn't own any horses, but he could see that changing very easily. After all, he didn't have dogs yet either.

A prayer ran through his mind that he could find clarity of thought as Collin asked, "What budget are we looking at?"

Todd didn't need to worry about money. He had plenty of that. The real question was whether or not he wanted neighbors close to him or a little more privacy. And after living in a row of tour buses and RVs for nineteen years, he decided he'd like a bit more freedom to walk around the house in the buff if he wanted to.

Not that he'd ever done that.

But he could if he wanted to.

"The budget is...I don't know. What kind of budget do I need for a house in the mountains somewhere? Maybe a bit away from the neighbor's but not too far from a grocery store."

Collin looked like he wanted to laugh again, but he didn't. His fingers flew over the keyboard, and he said, "Let's see what I've got."

A couple of hours later, Todd had seen three mountain houses, all of them with thousands and thousands of square feet he didn't need. At least not for just himself. Now, if he was planning a huge family reunion, the place on Prospect Bay Drive would be perfect, what with that boat dock right on the water's edge.

A headache pounded behind his right eye, a result of an injury during a bull ride from a decade ago. He disliked the pain that seemed to plague him at the most inopportune times, but he'd used his health to get out of sticky situations in the past too. Today, for example, he'd said he had a headache and asked Collin if they could do Househunting Round Two another day.

His cousin had readily agreed, pointed in the direction of the drug store as if Todd had never been to Coral Canyon before, and gone back inside to pull a new list of houses they'd look at later.

A week went by, and Todd never did go out with Collin again. He hung around the RV park, hiked a few trails in the surrounding area, and wondered if this quiet, retired life was what he really wanted.

Problem was, Todd had no idea what he wanted. And that was odd, as he'd grown up with a desire to become a champion bull-rider. And he had. He'd worked, and trained, and clung to that dream until it had come true.

He didn't mind the fame, and the fortune wasn't bad either, so he'd stayed in the circuit, surrounding by family and friends, until he'd felt it was time to leave.

He'd been lonely before, but this was a whole new level of being alone he hadn't experienced before. When he drove by the new billboard and saw his face up-close and in color on the twenty-foot sign, the breath left his body.

He definitely could not drive by that thing every day. "So a house up a different canyon," he said to himself. Then he wouldn't have to drive by that sign every time he needed bread.

At the gas station just inside city limits, he pulled behind a huge, boxy, black SUV, wondering if tourists came to Coral Canyon this early in April. Coral Canyon typically didn't get many tourists at all, at least not that Todd remembered.

But this didn't look like a vehicle that belonged in simple, humble Coral Canyon. A cowboy came out of the convenience store, whistling as if he was the happiest man

on earth. He carried a bag that looked full of chips and
candy, and Todd turned away to fill his own truck up
with gas.

Someone calling, "Graham! Graham Whittaker!" had
Todd spinning back. He watched as a woman handed him a
bottle of Gatorade and rushed back into the store. Graham
turned back to his SUV, and he glanced at Todd.

Their eyes locked, and Todd started laughing. "Graham
Whittaker." He left the pump and strode over to his childhood friend.

"Todd Christopherson." Graham grabbed onto him and
gave him several hearty slaps on the back as they embraced.
He stepped back and grinned. "It's great to see you. I didn't
know you were back in town."

"You haven't seen the huge billboard on the way in?"
Todd snorted. "It's embarrassing, that's what it is."

"Oh, I live up the canyon on the north," he said.

"That's where I need to be then," Todd said, his mind
searching into the past. "Isn't there just a lodge up there?"

"And a ranch," he said. "My wife's ranch. Echo Ridge?"

"Oh, right. The McAllister place. You married Laney?"

Graham had a happy, married-man glow about him. "Yep,
about five years ago." He opened the door of the SUV and
tossed in the bag of snacks. "And I bought the lodge too." He
cocked his head, clearly considering something.

Todd had seen that look in Graham's eyes before, and
usually nothing good came from it. "What?" he asked
carefully.

"What are you doin' these days?"

"Nothing," Todd said. Literally.

"We need help at the ranch. I don't suppose you'd be interested in something like that?"

Todd's heart leapt over itself. "I would," he said. At the very least, it would get him out of his bus and into the fresh air. "What kind of work?"

"Echo Ridge is a cattle ranch," Graham said. "We're down a man this year due to health problems, and we need someone to start pretty much yesterday."

"I can come out today," Todd said. Right now. He could follow Graham up that north canyon and wrangle cattle *right now*.

Graham smiled. "Where you livin'?"

"In my tour bus out at the RV park on the road toward Jackson."

Graham's eyebrows went sky high. "Oh, I need to see this tour bus."

Todd really liked that Graham wasn't falling all over him like he was a celebrity. Not that Todd minded that kind of attention. But it was nice to have a normal friend too. A familiar face who didn't act like he was somehow a different man because he'd won a few championships.

He chuckled. "I can drive it up to your ranch. Live in it while I work. Do you have water hookups?"

"Not at the ranch," he said. "The lodge might, actually. But you know, you could just live at the lodge." Those blue eyes sharpened again. "I mean, my brother—remember Beau?—and his wife live there, but they're on a tour of Europe for the next few months. And it's huge anyway. Even if you were there, they wouldn't know it."

"I don't need a free place to live," Todd said.

"Yeah, of course not," Graham said easily. "But we typically offer room and board for our cowboys. Not at the lodge, but this is a special circumstance." He pulled out his phone. "And I can find out if it has water hookups. If so, you could just use those and live in the bus."

Todd felt the sparkle of opportunity, and he didn't want to miss it. "Sure," he said. "Okay. You just tell me what you want me to do."

"Why don't you come up to the lodge?" Graham said. "I'll show you around, and we'll check on the water, and then you can decide." He tapped on his phone and lifted it to his ear. "Laney will be thrilled to have your help." He grinned and said, "Hey, baby," as he turned away from Todd and got behind the wheel of the SUV.

Todd pulled the now-finished hose out of his truck and got behind the wheel too, ready to follow Graham up the north canyon. He didn't need a job, but it sure would be nice to have something to do with his time. Something outdoors. Something with the animals he'd spent his life around.

As he followed Graham and set his truck up the canyon, he felt like something good was about to come in to his life —and this time, he wouldn't let it get away.

THE LODGE WAS DEFINITELY of the upscale, posh, where-rich-people-stay variety. He didn't remember the Whittakers being particularly wealthy growing up, but Graham had definitely struck something in order to be able to afford a place like this.

Todd parked in the circle drive, behind Graham, and looked at the beautiful wood front door.

Graham got out of the SUV, his phone still stuck to his ear, and Todd caught up to him just as he said, "Okay, thanks anyway, Will." He tucked his phone in his pocket and walked up the steps. "No water hookups here. But the lodge is nice, I promise."

He opened the front door and went inside. Todd wasn't disappointed. A beautiful stained glass window spelled out Graham's last name, and a sweeping staircase led up to the second floor. The spacious foyer gave way to a big living room with couches, chairs, and a fireplace.

"Living room." Graham moved through that to a door-way. "Kitchen back here." He went straight into the kitchen and stopped suddenly. "Who are you?"

Todd almost ran into him, but managed to stop and step to the side in time to see a woman with short, blonde hair standing in the kitchen. She held up a regular spoon as if she'd attack with it, and a smudge of chocolate sat in the corner of her mouth.

"Graham," she said at the same time he said, "Vi?"

"What are you doing here?" they said in unison, and Todd felt like he was watching a tennis match. He liked looking at Vi a lot more than Graham, and his gaze stuck on her the next time it moved to her.

If he had to categorize her, she'd be in the drop-dead gorgeous category, with fair skin, a smattering of freckles across her nose, and curves in all the right places. She licked her lips and put the spoon down, casually stepping in front of something on the counter.

And Todd really wanted to know what it was. Who *she* was. And if she could possibly be interested in a retired bull rider with no roots.

HER COWBOY BILLIONAIRE BULL RIDER, featuring Violet Everett and Todd Christopherson, a big-time champion billionaire bull rider, is coming on December 11.

Preorder now!

Her Cowboy Billionaire Best Friend (Book 1): Graham Whittaker returns to Coral Canyon a few days after Christmas—after the death of his father. He takes over the energy company his dad built from the ground up and buys a high-end lodge to live in—only a mile from the home of his once-best friend, Laney McAllister. They were best friends once, but Laney's always entertained feelings for him, and spending so much time with him while they make Christmas memories puts her heart in danger of getting broken again...

Her Cowboy Billionaire Boss (Book 2): Since the death of his wife a few years ago, Eli Whittaker has been running from one job to another, unable to find somewhere for him and his son to settle. Meg Palmer is Stockton's nanny, and she comes with her boss, Eli, to the lodge, her long-time crush on the man no different in Wyoming than it was on the beach. When she confesses her feelings for him and gets nothing in return, she's crushed, embarrassed, and unsure if she can stay in Coral Canyon for Christmas. Then Eli starts to show some feelings for her too...

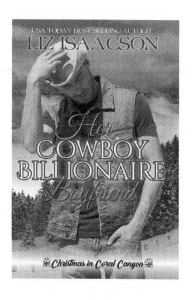

Her Cowboy Billionaire Boyfriend (Book 3): Andrew Whittaker is the public face for the Whittaker Brothers' family energy company, and with his older brother's robot about to be announced, he needs a press secretary to help him get everything ready and tour the state to make the announcements. When he's hit by a protest sign being carried by the company's biggest opponent, Rebecca Collings, he learns with a few clicks that she has the background they need. He offers her the job of press secretary when she thought she was going to be arrested, and not only because the spark between them in so hot Andrew can't see straight.

Can Becca and Andrew work together and keep their relationship a secret? Or will hearts break in this classic romance retelling reminiscent of *Two Weeks Notice*?

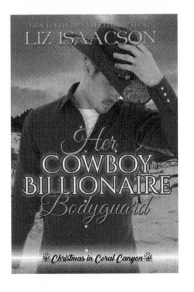

Her Cowboy Billionaire Bodyguard (Book 4): Beau Whittaker has watched his brothers find love one by one, but every attempt he's made has ended in disaster. Lily Everett has been in the spotlight since childhood and has half a dozen platinum records with her two sisters. She's taking a break from the brutal music industry and hiding out in Wyoming while her ex-husband continues to cause trouble for her. When she hears of Beau Whittaker and what he offers his clients, she wants to meet him. Beau is instantly attracted to Lily, but he tried a relationship with his last client that left a scar that still hasn't healed...

Can Lily use the spirit of Christmas to discover what matters most? Will Beau open his heart to the possibility of love with someone so different from him?

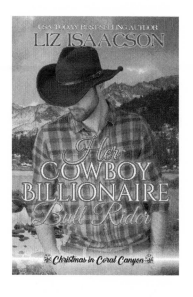

Her Cowboy Billionaire Bull Rider (Book 5): Todd Christopherson has just retired from the professional rodeo circuit and returned to his hometown of Coral Canyon. Problem is, he's got no family there anymore, no land, and no job. Not that he needs a job--he's got plenty of money from his illustrious career riding bulls.

Then Todd gets thrown during a routine horseback ride up the canyon, and his only support as he recovers physically is the beautiful Violet Everett. She's no nurse, but she does the best she can for the handsome cowboy. **Will she lose her heart to the billionaire bull rider? Can Todd trust that God led him to Coral Canyon...and Vi?**

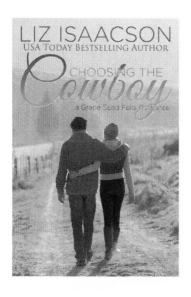

Choosing the Cowboy (Book 1): With financial trouble and personal issues around every corner, can Maggie Duffin and Chase Carver rely on their faith to find their happily-ever-after?

A spinoff from the #1 bestselling Three Rivers Ranch Romance novels, also by USA Today bestselling author Liz Isaacson.

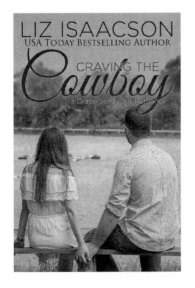

Craving the Cowboy (Book 2): Dwayne Carver is set to inherit his family's ranch in the heart of Texas Hill Country, and in order to keep up with his ranch duties and fulfill his dreams of owning a horse farm, he hires top trainer Felicity Lightburne. They get along great, and she can envision herself on this new farm—at least until her mother falls ill and she has to return to help her. Can Dwayne and Felicity work through their differences to find their happily-ever-after?

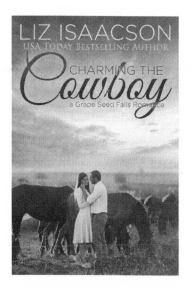

Charming the Cowboy (Book 3): Third grade teacher Heather Carver has had her eye on Levi Rhodes for a couple of years now, but he seems to be blind to her attempts to charm him. When she breaks her arm while on his horse ranch, Heather infiltrates Levi's life in ways he's never thought of, and his strict anti-female stance slips. Will Heather heal his emotional scars and he care for her physical ones so they can have a real relationship?

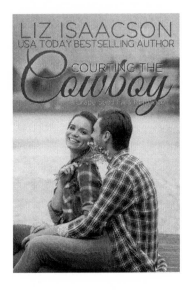

Courting the Cowboy (Book 4): Frustrated with the cowboy-only dating scene in Grape Seed Falls, May Sotheby joins TexasFaithful.com, hoping to find her soul mate without having to relocate--or deal with cowboy hats and boots. She has no idea that Kurt Pemberton, foreman at Grape Seed Ranch, is the man she starts communicating with... Will May be able to follow her heart and get Kurt to forgive her so they can be together?

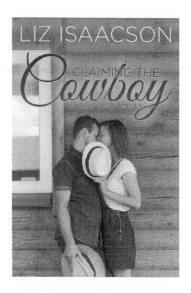

Claiming the Cowboy, Royal Brothers Book 1 (Grape Seed Falls Romance Book 5): Unwilling to be tied down, farrier Robin Cook has managed to pack her entire life into a two-hundred-and-eighty square-foot house, and that includes her Yorkie. Cowboy and co-foreman, Shane Royal has had his heart set on Robin for three years, even though she flat-out turned him down the last time he asked her to dinner. But she's back at Grape Seed Ranch for five weeks as she works her horseshoeing magic, and he's still interested, despite a bitter life lesson that left a bad taste for marriage in his mouth.

Robin's interested in him too. But can she find room for Shane in her tiny house--and can he take a chance on her with his tired heart?

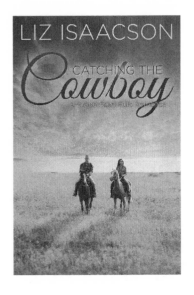

Catching the Cowboy, Royal Brothers Book 2 (Grape Seed Falls Romance Book 6): Dylan Royal is good at two things: whistling and caring for cattle. When his cows are being attacked by an unknown wild animal, he calls Texas Parks & Wildlife for help. He wasn't expecting a beautiful mammologist to show up, all flirty and fun and everything Dylan didn't know he wanted in his life.

Hazel Brewster has gone on more first dates than anyone in Grape Seed Falls, and she thinks maybe Dylan deserves a second... Can they find their way through wild animals, huge life changes, and their emotional pasts to find their forever future?

Cheering the Cowboy, Royal Brothers Book 3 (Grape Seed Falls Romance Book 7): Austin Royal loves his life on his new ranch with his brothers. But he doesn't love that Shayleigh Hatch came with the property, nor that he has to take the blame for the fact that he now owns her childhood ranch. They rarely have a conversation that doesn't leave him furious and frustrated--and yet he's still attracted to Shay in a strange, new way.

Shay inexplicably likes him too, which utterly confuses and angers her. As they work to make this Christmas the best the Triple Towers Ranch has ever seen, can they also navigate through their rocky relationship to smoother waters?

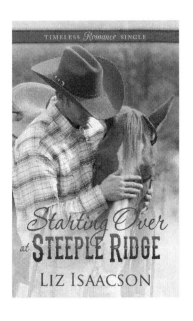

Starting Over at Steeple Ridge: Steeple Ridge Romance (Book 1): Tucker Jenkins has had enough of tall buildings, traffic, and has traded in his technology firm in New York City for Steeple Ridge Horse Farm in rural Vermont. Missy Marino has worked at the farm since she was a teen, and she's always dreamed of owning it. But her ex-husband left her with a truckload of debt, making her fantasies of owning the farm unfulfilled. Tucker didn't come to the country to find a new wife, but he supposes a woman could help him start over in Steeple Ridge. Will Tucker and Missy be able to navigate the shaky ground between them to find a new beginning?

Finding Love at Steeple Ridge: A Butters Brothers Novel, Steeple Ridge Romance (Book 2): Ben Buttars is the youngest of the four Buttars brothers who come to Steeple Ridge Farm, and he finally feels like he's landed somewhere he can make a life for himself. Reagan Cantwell is a decade older than Ben and the recreational direction for the town of Island Park. Though Ben is young, he knows what he wants—and that's Rae. Can she figure out how to put what matters most in her life—family and faith—above her job before she loses Ben?

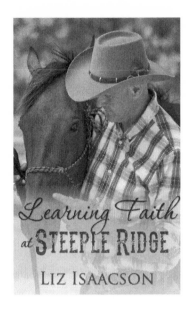

Learning Faith at Steeple Ridge: A Butters Brothers Novel, Steeple Ridge Romance (Book 3): Sam Buttars has spent the last decade making sure he and his brothers stay together. They've been at Steeple Ridge for a while now, but with the youngest married and happy, the siren's call to return to his parents' farm in Wyoming is loud in Sam's ears. He'd just go if it weren't for beautiful Bonnie Sherman, who roped his heart the first time he saw her. Do Sam and Bonnie have the faith to find comfort in each other instead of in the people who've already passed?

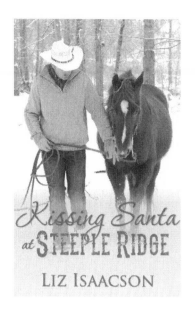

Learning Faith at Steeple Ridge: A Butters Brothers Novel, Steeple Ridge Romance (Book 4): Logan Buttars has always been good-natured and happy-go-lucky. After watching two of his brothers settle down, he recognizes a void in his life he didn't know about. Veterinarian Layla Guyman has appreciated Logan's friendship and easy way with animals when he comes into the clinic to get the service dogs. But with his future at Steeple Ridge in the balance, she's not sure a relationship with him is worth the risk. Can she rely on her faith and employ patience to tame Logan's wild heart?

Learning Faith at Steeple Ridge: A Butters Brothers Novel, Steeple Ridge Romance (Book 5): Darren Buttars is cool, collected, and quiet—and utterly devastated when his girlfriend of nine months, Farrah Irvine, breaks up with him because he wanted her to ride her horse in a parade. But Farrah doesn't ride anymore, a fact she made very clear to Darren. She returned to her childhood home with so much baggage, she doesn't know where to start with the unpacking. Darren's the only Buttars brother who isn't married, and he wants to make Island Park his permanent home—with Farrah. Can they find their way through the heartache to achieve a happily-ever-after together?

After the Fall: A Gold Valley Romance (Book 2): Professional snowboarder Sterling Maughan has sequestered himself in his family's cabin in the exclusive mountain community above Gold Valley, Montana after a devastating fall that ended his career. Norah Watson cleans Sterling's cabin and the more time they spend together, the more Sterling is interested in all things Norah. As his body heals, so does his faith. Will Norah be able to trust Sterling so they can have a chance at true love?

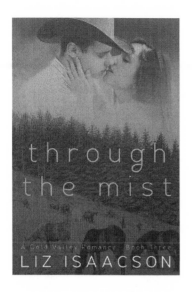

Through the Mist: A Gold Valley Romance (Book 3): Landon Edmunds has been a cowboy his whole life. An accident five years ago ended his successful rodeo career, and now he's looking to start a horse ranch--and he's looking outside of Montana. Which would be great if God hadn't brought Megan Palmer back to Gold Valley right when Landon is looking to leave. Megan and Landon work together well, and as sparks fly, she's sure God brought her back to Gold Valley so she could find her happily ever after. Through serious discussion and prayer, can Landon and Megan find their future together?

Be sure to check out the spinoff series, the Brush Creek Brides romances after you read THROUGH THE MIST. Start with A WEDDING FOR THE WIDOWER.

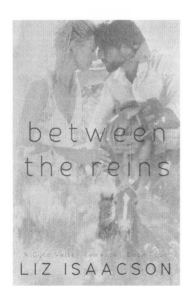

Between the Reins: A Gold Valley Romance (Book 4): Twelve years ago, Owen Carr left Gold Valley—and his long-time girlfriend—in favor of a country music career in Nashville. Married and divorced, Natalie teaches ballet at the dance studio in Gold Valley, but she never auditioned for the professional company the way she dreamed of doing. With Owen back, she realizes all the opportunities she missed out on when he left all those years ago—including a future with him. Can they mend broken bridges in order to have a second chance at love?

Over the Moon: A Gold Valley Romance (Book 5): Caleb Chamberlain has spent the last five years recovering from a horrible breakup, his alcoholism that stemmed from it, and the car accident that left him hospitalized. He's finally on the right track in his life—until Holly Gray, his twin brother's ex-fiance mistakes him for Nathan. Holly's back in Gold Valley to get the required veterinarian hours to apply for her graduate program. When the herd at Horseshoe Home comes down with pneumonia, Caleb and Holly are forced to work together in close quarters. Holly's over Nathan, but she hasn't forgiven him—or the woman she believes broke up their relationship. Can Caleb and Holly navigate such a rough past to find their happily-ever-after?

Journey to Steeple Ridge Farm with Holly—and fall in love with the cowboys there in the Steeple Ridge Romance series! Start with STARTING OVER AT STEEPLE RIDGE.

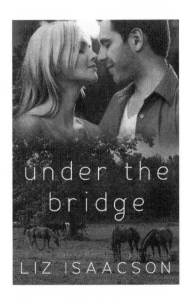

Under the Bridge: A Gold Valley Romance (Book 6): Ty Barker has been dancing through the last thirty years of his life--and he's suddenly realized he's alone. River Lee Whitely is back in Gold Valley with her two little girls after a divorce that's left deep scars. She has a job at Silver Creek that requires her to be able to ride a horse, and she nearly tramples Ty at her first lesson. That's just fine by him, because River Lee is the girl Ty has never gotten over. Ty realizes River Lee needs time to settle into her new job, her new home, her new life as a single parent, but going slow has never been his style. But for River Lee, can Ty take the necessary steps to keep her in his life?

Up on the Housetop: A Gold Valley Romance (Book 7): Archer Bailey has already lost one job to Emersyn Enders, so he deliberately doesn't tell her about the cowhand job up at Horseshoe Home Ranch. Emery's temporary job is ending, but her obligations to her physically disabled sister aren't. As Archer and Emery work together, its clear that the sparks flying between them aren't all from their friendly competition over a job. Will Emery and Archer be able to navigate the ranch, their close quarters, and their individual circumstances to find love this holiday season?

Around the Bend: A Gold Valley Romance (Book 8): Cowboy Elliott Hawthorne has just lost his best friend and cabin mate to the worst thing imaginable—marriage. When his brother calls about an accident with their father, Elliott rushes down to Gold Valley from the ranch only to be met with the most beautiful woman he's ever seen. His father's new physical therapist, London Marsh, likes the handsome face and gentle spirit she sees in Elliott too. Can Elliott and London navigate difficult family situations to find a happily-ever-after?

Second Chance Ranch: A Three Rivers Ranch Romance (Book 1): After his deployment, injured and discharged Major Squire Ackerman returns to Three Rivers Ranch, wanting to forgive Kelly for ignoring him a decade ago. He'd like to provide the stable life she needs, but with old wounds opening and a ranch on the brink of financial collapse, it will take patience and faith to make their second chance possible.

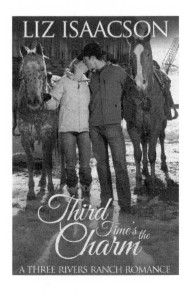

Third Time's the Charm: A Three Rivers Ranch Romance (Book 2): First Lieutenant Peter Marshall has a truckload of debt and no way to provide for a family, but Chelsea helps him see past all the obstacles, all the scars. With so many unknowns, can Pete and Chelsea develop the love, acceptance, and faith needed to find their happily ever after?

Fourth and Long: A Three Rivers Ranch Romance (Book 3): Commander Brett Murphy goes to Three Rivers Ranch to find some rest and relaxation with his Army buddies. Having his ex-wife show up with a seven-year-old she claims is his son is anything but the R&R he craves. Kate needs to make amends, and Brett needs to find forgiveness, but are they too late to find their happily ever after?

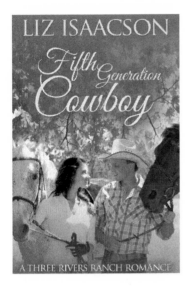

Fifth Generation Cowboy: A Three Rivers Ranch Romance (Book 4): Tom Lovell has watched his friends find their true happiness on Three Rivers Ranch, but everywhere he looks, he only sees friends. Rose Reyes has been bringing her daughter out to the ranch for equine therapy for months, but it doesn't seem to be working. Her challenges with Mari are just as frustrating as ever. Could Tom be exactly what Rose needs? Can he remove his friendship blinders and find love with someone who's been right in front of him all this time?

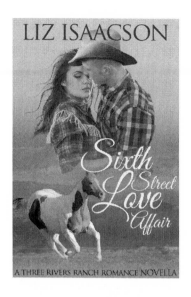

LIZ ISAACSON

Sixth Street Love Affair

A THREE RIVERS RANCH ROMANCE NOVELLA

Sixth Street Love Affair: A Three Rivers Ranch Romance (Book 5): After losing his wife a few years back, Garth Ahlstrom thinks he's ready for a second chance at love. But Juliette Thompson has a secret that could destroy their budding relationship. Can they find the strength, patience, and faith to make things work?

The Seventh Sergeant: A Three Rivers Ranch Romance (Book 6): Life has finally started to settle down for Sergeant Reese Sanders after his devastating injury overseas. Discharged from the Army and now with a good job at Courage Reins, he's finally found happiness—until a horrific fall puts him right back where he was years ago: Injured and depressed. Carly Watters, Reese's new veteran care coordinator, dislikes small towns almost as much as she loathes cowboys. But she finds herself faced with both when she gets assigned to Reese's case. Do they have the humility and faith to make their relationship more than professional?

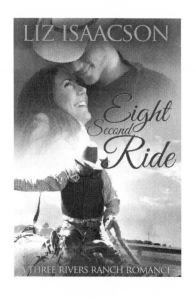

Eight Second Ride: A Three Rivers Ranch Romance (Book 7): Ethan Greene loves his work at Three Rivers Ranch, but he can't seem to find the right woman to settle down with. When sassy yet vulnerable Brynn Bowman shows up at the ranch to recruit him back to the rodeo circuit, he takes a different approach with the barrel racing champion. His patience and newfound faith pay off when a friendship--and more--starts with Brynn. But she wants out of the rodeo circuit right when Ethan wants to rejoin. Can they find the path God wants them to take and still stay together?

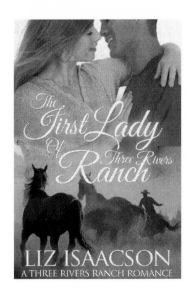

The First Lady of Three Rivers Ranch: A Three Rivers Ranch Romance (Book 8): Heidi Duffin has been dreaming about opening her own bakery since she was thirteen years old. She scrimped and saved for years to afford baking and pastry school in San Francisco. And now she only has one year left before she's a certified pastry chef. Frank Ackerman's father has recently retired, and he's taken over the largest cattle ranch in the Texas Panhandle. A horseman through and through, he's also nearing thirty-one and looking for someone to bring love and joy to a homestead that's been dominated by men for a decade. But when he convinces Heidi to come clean the cowboy cabins, she changes all that. But the siren's call of a bakery is still loud in Heidi's ears, even if she's also seeing a future with Frank. Can she rely on her faith in ways she's never had to before or will their relationship end when summer does?

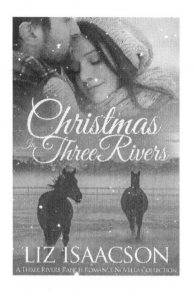

Christmas in Three Rivers: A Three Rivers Ranch Romance (Book 9): Isn't Christmas the best time to fall in love? The cowboys of Three Rivers Ranch think so. Join four of them as they journey toward their path to happily ever after in four, all-new novellas in the Amazon #1 Bestselling Three Rivers Ranch Romance series.

THE NINTH INNING: The Christmas season has never felt like such a burden to boutique owner Andrea Larsen. But with Mama gone and the holidays upon her, Andy finds herself wishing she hadn't been so quick to judge her former boyfriend, cowboy Lawrence Collins. Well, Lawrence hasn't forgotten about Andy either, and he devises a plan to get her out to the ranch so they can reconnect. Do they have the faith and humility to patch things up and start a new relationship?

TEN DAYS IN TOWN: Sandy Keller is tired of the dating scene in Three Rivers. Though she owns the pancake house, she's looking for a fresh start, which means an escape from the town where she grew up. When her older brother's best friend, Tad Jorgensen, comes to town for the holidays, it is a balm to his weary soul. A helicopter tour guide who experi-

enced a near-death experience, he's looking to start over too-
-but in Three Rivers. Can Sandy and Tad navigate their troubles to find the path God wants them to take--and discover
true love--in only ten days?

ELEVEN YEAR REUNION: Pastry chef extraordinaire,
Grace Lewis has moved to Three Rivers to help Heidi
Ackerman open a bakery in Three Rivers. Grace relishes the
idea of starting over in a town where no one knows about
her failed cupcakery. She doesn't expect to run into her old
high school boyfriend, Jonathan Carver. A carpenter working
at Three Rivers Ranch, Jon's in town against his will. But
with Grace now on the scene, Jon's thinking life in Three
Rivers is suddenly looking up. But with her focus on baking
and his disdain for small towns, can they make their eleven
year reunion stick?

THE TWELFTH TOWN: Newscaster Taryn Tucker has
had enough of life on-screen. She's bounced from town to
town before arriving in Three Rivers, completely alone and
completely anonymous--just the way she now likes it. She
takes a job cleaning at Three Rivers Ranch, hoping for a
chance to figure out who she is and where God wants her.
When she meets happy-go-lucky cowhand Kenny Stockton,
she doesn't expect sparks to fly. Kenny's always been "the
best friend" for his female friends, but the pull between him
and Taryn can't be denied. Will they have the courage and
faith necessary to make their opposite worlds mesh?

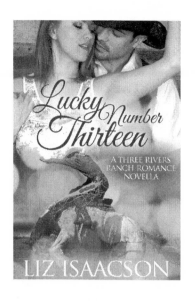

Lucky Number Thirteen: A Three Rivers Ranch Romance (Book 10): Tanner Wolf, a rodeo champion ten times over, is excited to be riding in Three Rivers for the first time since he left his philandering ways and found religion. Seeing his old friends Ethan and Brynn is therapuetic--until a terrible accident lands him in the hospital. With his rodeo career over, Tanner thinks maybe he'll stay in town--and it's not just because his nurse, Summer Hamblin, is the prettiest woman he's ever met. But Summer's the queen of first dates, and as she looks for a way to make a relationship with the transient rodeo star work Summer's not sure she has the fortitude to go on a second date. Can they find love among the tragedy?

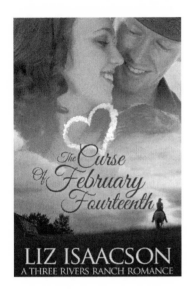

The Curse of February Fourteenth: A Three Rivers Ranch Romance (Book 11): Cal Hodgkins, cowboy veterinarian at Bowman's Breeds, isn't planning to meet anyone at the masked dance in small-town Three Rivers. He just wants to get his bachelor friends off his back and sit on the sidelines to drink his punch. But when he sees a woman dressed in gorgeous butterfly wings and cowgirl boots with blue stitching, he's smitten. Too bad she runs away from the dance before he can get her name, leaving only her boot behind...

Fifteen Minutes of Fame: A Three Rivers Ranch Romance (Book 12): Navy Richards is thirty-five years of tired—tired of dating the same men, working a demanding job, and getting her heart broken over and over again. Her aunt has always spoken highly of the matchmaker in Three Rivers, Texas, so she takes a six-month sabbatical from her high-stress job as a pediatric nurse, hops on a bus, and meets with the matchmaker. Then she meets Gavin Redd. He's handsome, he's hardworking, and he's a cowboy. But is he an Aquarius too? Navy's not making a move until she knows for sure...

Sixteen Steps to Fall in Love: A Three Rivers Ranch Romance (Book 13): A chance encounter at a dog park sheds new light on the tall, talented Boone that Nicole can't ignore. As they get to know each other better and start to dig into each other's past, Nicole is the one who wants to run. This time from her growing admiration and attachment to Boone. From her aging parents. From herself.

But Boone feels the attraction between them too, and he decides he's tired of running and ready to make Three Rivers his permanent home. **Can Boone and Nicole use their faith to overcome their differences and find a happily-ever-after together?**

The Sleigh on Seventeenth Street: A Three Rivers Ranch Romance (Book 14): A cowboy with skills as an electrician tries a relationship with a down-on-her luck plumber. Can Dylan and Camila make water and electricity play nicely together this Christmas season? Or will they get shocked as they try to make their relationship work?

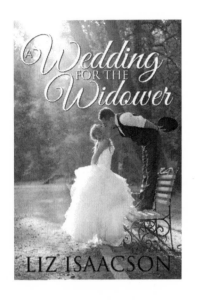

A Wedding for the Widower: Brush Creek Brides Romance (Book 1): Former rodeo champion and cowboy Walker Thompson trains horses at Brush Creek Horse Ranch, where he lives a simple life in his cabin with his ten-year-old son. A widower of six years, he's worked with Tess Wagner, a widow who came to Brush Creek to escape the turmoil of her life to give her seven-year-old son a slower pace of life. But Tess's breast cancer is back...

Walker will have to decide if he'd rather spend even a short time with Tess than not have her in his life at all. Tess wants to feel God's love and power, but can she discover and accept God's will in order to find her happy ending?

A Companion for the Cowboy: Brush Creek Brides Romance (Book 2): Cowboy and professional roper Justin Jackman has found solitude at Brush Creek Horse Ranch, preferring his time with the animals he trains over dating. With two failed engagements in his past, he's not really interested in getting his heart stomped on again. But when flirty and fun 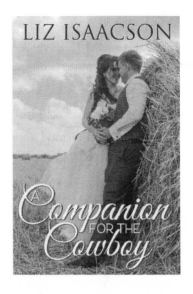 Renee Martin picks him up at a church ice cream bar--on a bet, no less--he finds himself more than just a little interested. His Gen-X attitudes are attractive to her; her Millennial behaviors drive him nuts. Can Justin look past their differences and take a chance on another engagement?

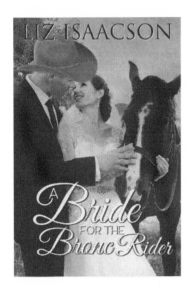

A Bride for the Bronc Rider: Brush Creek Brides Romance (Book 3): Ted Caldwell has been a retired bronc rider for years, and he thought he was perfectly happy training horses to buck at Brush Creek Ranch. He was wrong. When he meets April Nox, who comes to the ranch to hide her pregnancy from all her friends back in Jackson Hole, Ted realizes he has a huge family-shaped hole in his life. April is embarrassed, heartbroken, and trying to find her extinguished faith. She's never ridden a horse and wants nothing to do with a cowboy ever again. Can Ted and April create a family of happiness and love from a tragedy?

A Family for the Farmer: Brush Creek Brides Romance (Book 4): Blake Gibbons oversees all the agriculture at Brush Creek Horse Ranch, sometimes moonlighting as a general contractor. When he meets Erin Shields, new in town, at her aunt's bakery, he's instantly smitten. Erin moved to Brush Creek after a divorce that left her penniless, homeless, and a

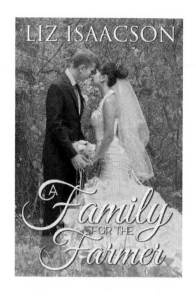

single mother of three children under age eight. She's nowhere near ready to start dating again, but the longer Blake hangs around the bakery, the more she starts to like him. Can Blake and Erin find a way to blend their lifestyles and become a family?

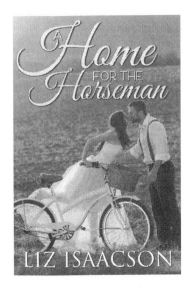

A Home for the Horseman: Brush Creek Brides Romance (Book 5): Emmett Graves has always had a positive outlook on life. He adores training horses to become barrel racing champions during the day and cuddling with his cat at night. Fresh off her professional rodeo retirement, Molly Brady comes to Brush Creek Horse Ranch as Emmett's protege. He's not thrilled, and she's allergic to cats. Oh, and she'd like to stay cowboy-free, thank you very much. But Emmett's about as cowboy as they come.... Can Emmett and Molly work together without falling in love?

A Refuge for the Rancher: Brush Creek Brides Romance (Book 6): Grant Ford spends his days training cattle—when he's not camped out at the elementary school hoping to catch a glimpse of his ex-girlfriend. When principal Shannon Sharpe confronts him and asks him to stay away from the school, the spark between them is instant and hot. Shannon's expecting 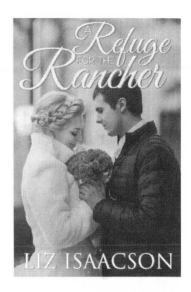 a transfer very soon, but she also needs a summer outdoor coordinator—and Grant fits the bill. Just because he's handsome and everything Shannon's ever wanted in a cowboy husband means nothing. Will Grant and Shannon be able to survive the summer or will the Utah heat be too much for them to handle?

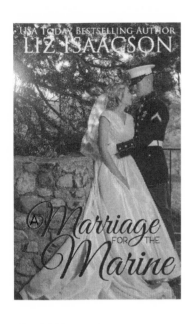

A Marriage for the Marine: A Fuller Family Novel - Brush Creek Brides Romance (Book 7): Tate Benson can't believe he's come to Nowhere, Utah, to fix up a house that hasn't been inhabited in years. But he has. Because he's retired from the Marines and looking to start a life as a police officer in small-town Brush Creek. Wren Fuller has her hands full most days running her family's company. When Tate calls and demands a maid for that morning, she decides to have the calls forwarded to her cell and go help him out. She didn't know he was moving in next door, and she's completely unprepared for his handsomeness, his kind heart, and his wounded soul.Can Tate and Wren weather a relationship when they're also next-door neighbors?

A Fiancé for the Fire-fighter: A Fuller Family Novel - Brush Creek Brides Romance (Book 8): Cora Wesley comes to Brush Creek, hoping to get some in-the-wild firefighting training as she prepares to put in her application to be a hotshot. When she meets Brennan Fuller, the spark between them is hot and instant. As they get to know each other,

her deadline is constantly looming over them, and Brennan starts to wonder if he can break ranks in the family business. He's okay mowing lawns and hanging out with his brothers, but he dreams of being able to go to college and become a landscape architect, but he's just not sure it can be done. Will Cora and Brennan be able to endure their trials to find true love?

A Treasure for the Trooper: A Fuller Family Novel - Brush Creek Brides Romance (Book 9): Dawn Fuller has made some mistakes in her life, and she's not proud of the way McDermott Boyd found her off the road one day last year. She's spent a hard year wrestling with her choices and trying to fix them, glad for McDermott's acceptance and friendship. He lost his wife years ago, done his best with his daughter, and now he's ready to move on. Can McDermott help Dawn find a way past her former mistakes and down a path that leads to love, family, and happiness?

A Date for the Detective: A Fuller Family Novel - Brush Creek Brides Romance (Book 10): Dahlia Reid is one of the best detectives Brush Creek and the surrounding towns has ever had. She's given up on the idea of marriage—and pleasing her mother—and has dedicated herself fully to her job. Which is great, since one of the most perplexing cases of her career

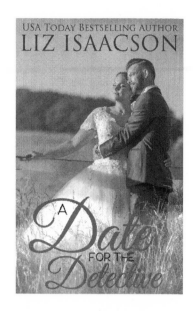

has come to town. Kyler Fuller thinks he's finally ready to move past the woman who ghosted him years ago. He's cut his hair, and he's ready to start dating. Too bad every woman he's been out with is about as interesting as a lamppost—until Dahlia. He finds her beautiful, her quick wit a breath of fresh air, and her intelligence sexy. Can Kyler and Dahlia use their faith to find a way through the obstacles threatening to keep them apart?

A Partner for the Paramedic: A Fuller Family Novel - Brush Creek Brides Romance (Book 11): Jazzy Fuller has always been overshadowed by her prettier, more popular twin, Fabiana. Fabi meets paramedic Max Robinson at the park and sets a date with him only to come down with the flu. So she convinces Jazzy to cut her hair and take her place on the date. And the spark between Jazzy and Max is hot and instant...if only he knew she wasn't her sister, Fabi.

Max drives the ambulance for the town of Brush Creek with is partner Ed Moon, and neither of them have been all that lucky in love. Until Max suggests to who he thinks is Fabi that they should double with Ed and Jazzy. They do, and Fabi is smitten with the steady, strong Ed Moon. As each twin falls further and further in love with their respective paramedic, it becomes obvious they'll need to come clean about the switcheroo sooner rather than later...or risk losing their hearts.

A Catch for the Chief: A Fuller Family Novel - Brush Creek Brides Romance (Book 12): Berlin Fuller has struck out with the dating scene in Brush Creek more times than she cares to admit. When she makes a deal with her friends that they can choose the next man she goes out with, she didn't dream they'd pick surly Cole Fairbanks, the new Chief of Police. Not only is Cole twelve years older than Berlin, he doesn't date. Period.

His friends call him the Beast and challenge him to complete ten dates that summer or give up his bonus check. When Berlin approaches him, stuttering about the deal with her friends and claiming they don't actually have to go out, he's intrigued. As the summer passes, Cole finds himself burning both ends of the candle to keep up with his job and his new relationship. When he unleashes the Beast one time too many, Berlin will have to decide if she can tame him or if she should walk away.

ABOUT LIZ

Liz Isaacson writes inspirational romance, usually set in Texas, or Montana, or anywhere else horses and cowboys exist. She lives in Utah, where she teaches elementary school, taxis her daughter to dance several times a week, and eats a lot of Ferrero Rocher while writing. Find her on her website at lizisaacson.com.